New Orleans Revealed: 1838-1839
A Time Traveler's Handbook

Derrick Fitzgerald

Table of Contents

Welcome to the Retrorsum Time Travel Book Series

••••

New Orleans Revealed: 1838-1839-Introduction:

The following is a comprehensive guide and promotional material for the *Retrorsum Time Travel Book Series* by Derrick Fitzgerald. Within its pages, you will discover a wealth of valuable information meticulously gathered to assist you in your hypothetical journey to New Orleans, Louisiana, during the Antebellum years of 1838–1839. Every detail presented is authentic, encompassing essential guidance on preparation, accommodations, dining establishments, cafes, and the vibrant social venues that defined this fascinating period in American history.

In the previous installment, *Las Vegas Revealed*, the handbook referenced book one of *Retrorsum* and the remarkable experiences of Will Patterson in early 1930s Las Vegas. This guide, however, shifts focus to book three, *Las Vegas Revisited*. Here, the narrative expands beyond the great depression, prohibition and challenges of 1930s Las Vegas to include a daring rescue mission to late 1830s America. Will Patterson must embark on a 14 month perilous journey to rescue his close friend and former history professor, Charles Damron, who has inadvertently been thrust into an elongated mission to 1830s America. The stakes are higher than ever as Will navigates the complexities of this earlier time period, blending historical insight with thrilling adventure.

As before, while this guide does not claim to explain the mechanics of time travel to Antebellum New Orleans, it serves as an invaluable resource for those who, in the realm of possibility, find themselves able to traverse temporal boundaries successfully and arrive in the late 1830s. Should such an extraordinary journey be feasible, the insights provided herein could significantly enhance your experience and ensure your seamless integration into the vibrant and complex life of 1830s New Orleans. From the intricate architecture and bustling marketplaces to the lively gatherings in coffee houses and social clubs, this guide seeks to immerse you in the era, equipping you with the knowledge to make the most of your remarkable journey.

Late 1830s New Orleans is a universe away, even compared to the "relative" modernity of 1930s Las Vegas. For any temporal explorers, the shocking contrasts between the two eras will be unavoidable. New Orleans of this period is raw, primitive, and at times brutally unapologetic. This journey is not for the fainthearted or squeamish—1830s New Orleans is a city of extremes, where breathtaking cultural and architectural achievements coexist with inhuman practices and stark societal divisions.

At the height of its prominence, New Orleans was a thriving hub of commerce and culture, strategically situated along the Mississippi River. Its wharves teemed with activity, as ships arrived from across the globe carrying goods and, tragically, enslaved individuals. This city was not just the capital of trade but also the capital of the domestic slave market in the Antebellum South. Enslaved people were brought to the city en masse, housed in squalid slave pens, and sold in public auctions that reduced human lives to mere commodities. Families were routinely separated without hesitation, the cruel machinery of slavery grinding relentlessly beneath the surface of New Orleans' prosperity.

For travelers, navigating New Orleans in 1838–1839 offers both an immersive experience in cultural brilliance and an unflinching confrontation with its darkest realities. Gallatin Street, notorious for its clandestine bars, gambling dens, and brothels, epitomizes the city's unregulated edge. These shadowy establishments, with their raw violence and unchecked vice, echo the same cruelty and dehumanization found in the slave markets and pens, where the brutality of the era is laid bare. Together, Gallatin Street and the slave auctions reveal a world as shocking to any temporal visitor as it is formative to the city's history—cruel, merciless and unapologetically raw.

Amid these societal complexities, New Orleans also showcased its grandeur through its architectural marvels, particularly its hotels. One of the most striking symbols of the era was the fierce rivalry between the St. Charles and Verandah Hotels, which mirrored the ethnic and social tensions of the time. Located on opposite corners of St. Charles Street (now Avenue) and Common Street in what was then the Faubourg St. Mary, these two hotels represented the ambitions and divisions of the city's Anglo-American elite.

The St. Charles Hotel, opened in 1837, was a towering achievement of design and ambition. Spearheaded by a group of Anglo investors seeking to secure prestige for the American sector of New Orleans, the hotel was the vision of architects James Gallier Sr. and Charles Dakin. With its five-story grandeur and a 185-foot dome—the tallest point in the region—it quickly became a cultural and commercial cornerstone for the city's Anglo-American population. Lavish gatherings, elegant dinners, and grand social events made the St. Charles a beacon of high society.

Yet, the harmony of the St. Charles' backers was short-lived. Tensions at one investor celebration boiled over into insults, with toasts escalating into nationalistic retorts. What began as a convivial evening devolved into a heated exchange, culminating in a challenge issued by English-born Richard Owen Pritchard, who, incensed by his Irish counterparts, declared, "Damn your hotel! I will build one of my own!" True to his word, Pritchard financed the construction of the Verandah Hotel across the street, sparking a direct rivalry that mirrored the broader ethnic and social divides of the city.

The Verandah Hotel, though less monumental than the St. Charles, was no less ambitious in its intent. Designed as a direct competitor, it quickly established itself as a hub for Anglo-American elites who favored its refined but less ostentatious atmosphere. The rivalry between these two establishments epitomized the clashing identities within New Orleans, with each hotel serving as a symbol of the city's fragmented cultural, political, and economic realms.

While these grand hotels embodied the aspirations of their patrons, they also served as stark reminders of the privilege and wealth built on the backs of enslaved labor. Many of the skilled hands that constructed the St. Charles and the Verandah belonged to enslaved individuals, whose contributions went unrecognized while their suffering underpinned the city's prosperity.

Compared to the orderly, burgeoning modernity of 1930s Las Vegas, New Orleans in the late 1830s will feel anarchic and unrestrained. Public health crises like yellow fever and cholera ravaged the city, exacerbated by poor sanitation and crowded living conditions. Social hierarchies were rigidly enforced, yet the city thrived as a melting pot of cultural influences, blending Creole, Anglo, African, and European traditions into a uniquely vibrant identity. Theaters, masked balls, and music halls celebrated this cultural richness, even as the horrors of slavery and the struggles of the working class cast long shadows.

For temporal explorers, New Orleans in 1838–1839 offers an unparalleled journey into a world of contrasts—grandeur and squalor, refinement and brutality, hope and despair. From the opulent halls of the St. Charles Hotel to the unrestrained energy of Gallatin Street, the city demands resilience and an open mind. It is a place where the beauty of human achievement is inextricably tied to its moral contradictions, leaving no traveler unchanged by the experience.

In book three, *Las Vegas Revisited*, both Will Patterson and Charles Damron take up residence at the St. Charles Hotel, later followed by

Will Patterson's extended stay at the Verandah Hotel. For the temporal visitor, these two establishments provide a rare glimpse of relative modernity in a world that otherwise feels light-years removed from the present day. They serve as more than just accommodations—they are sanctuaries of relative comfort in a time marked by stark contrasts between refinement and the harsh realities of the Antebellum South.

The St. Charles Hotel, with its imposing five stories and 185-foot dome, stands as a monument to ambition and luxury. It offers near-modern amenities—running water, private baths, and cleanliness rare in this bustling southern city. The Verandah Hotel, though less grand than the St. Charles, provides similar comforts in a quieter, more understated setting, catering to affluent guests. Both embody the height of sophistication, serving plantation owners, politicians, industrialists, and the occasional time traveler seeking familiarity amidst the strangeness of the 1830s.

These hotels reflect the divisions and ambitions of Antebellum New Orleans. The St. Charles, in the American sector, showcases Anglo-American power, while the nearby Verandah arose from rivalry and ambition, mirroring the city's competitive spirit. Their refinement stands in sharp contrast to the chaos of Gallatin Street or the horrifying slave markets, which expose the darker realities behind the city's prosperity.

For the temporal traveler, staying at these hotels offers not only respite but also insight. To walk their corridors is to witness a microcosm of Antebellum New Orleans—a world where luxury and progress exist uneasily beside oppression and inequality. Even in polished settings, history's undercurrents remain palpable, revealing the complexities of 1830s life.

The Antebellum South: 1838-1839

A Journey to the Antebellum South: Insights for Temporal Explorers:

For any visitor from the 21st century or beyond, the Antebellum South of the late 1830s offers a world starkly different from modern life. Marked by extremes—opulent wealth and crushing poverty, a few bustling cities with New Orleans as its pinnacle, and many rural farms with virtually no modernity—it is a time of profound contrasts, with the pervasive inhumanity of slavery standing as its most tragic and disturbing feature.

Absence of Modern Conveniences:

Temporal visitors will be struck by the lack of modern amenities. Electricity, cars, telephones, and indoor plumbing are non-existent. (The St. Louis, St. Charles, and the Verandah were notable exceptions with regard to plumbing.) Lighting comes from candles or oil lamps, heating from fireplaces, and water must be manually drawn from wells. Everyday tasks like washing clothes or preserving food require intensive labor. Without refrigeration, methods such as salting, drying, or canning are essential for food storage.

Health and Medicine:

Medical care in the 1830s is rudimentary. Diseases like scarlet fever, cholera, and yellow fever are common, with treatments often ineffective or dangerous. Antibiotics and vaccines do not exist, and childbirth is fraught with peril. Temporal explorers who fall ill may find themselves at the mercy of primitive practices, highlighting the stark differences in healthcare across centuries.

Self-Sufficiency and Simplicity:

The era is often romanticized for its simplicity and self-reliance. Farmers, craftsmen, and laborers depended on their skills and communities, repairing and repurposing tools rather than discarding them. While plantation life reveals enormous self-sufficiency, its foundation rested on slave labor, which spared plantation owners from many of the era's hardships by forcing the enslaved to undergo them.

Societal Contrasts:

The inequalities of the Antebellum South are among its most jarring aspects. Wealthy elites lived in grandeur, their opulence built on the exploitation of enslaved labor. In contrast, many citizens struggled in poverty, relying on hard labor or small-scale farming. This contrasting of elegance and brutality underscores the contradictions of the time.

．．．．

A Mixed Experience:

Some visitors may appreciate the slower pace and absence of modern distractions, finding solace in the rhythms of nature and community. However, this simplicity is offset by grueling labor, rigid social hierarchies, and the moral weight of slavery.

Key Takeaways:

Antebellum New Orleans embodies stark contradictions: breathtaking architecture alongside squalor, vibrant culture shadowed by slavery. While modern comforts are absent, the resilience and ingenuity of the era's inhabitants provide valuable insights into humanity's adaptability. For the open-minded time traveler, this period offers a transformative glimpse into the roots of modern America, its achievements, and its scars.

New Orleans Revealed: 1838-1839- Preparation

Arrival-Protocols:

As detailed in *Las Vegas Revealed*, your point of arrival in 1830s New Orleans will likely differ significantly from that of 1930s Las Vegas. While 1930s Las Vegas benefits from vast tracts of empty desert ideal for safe and anonymous arrivals, New Orleans in the late 1830s is surrounded by low-lying swamps and wetlands, offering fewer isolated areas for discreet entry into this bustling city. In Book Three of *Retrorsum*, Will Patterson avoids arriving directly in 1830s New Orleans, instead traveling there from an alternate arrival point in New York City. His departure, however, from New Orleans was made possible only after rigorous testing conducted by the lab in Providence, RI, ensuring a safe and unobserved exit location. Multible drone fly-throughs were conducted to assure the exact moment of departure would be free of pedestrians and onlookers.

Temporal travelers must take similar precautions for both arrival and departure in New Orleans. Extensive testing will likely be necessary to identify a location—probably within the city itself—that will be free of potential onlookers at the precise moment of your arrival. Ideally, this should be a quiet, unlit street, alleyway, or other area with minimal foot traffic.

Once you arrive, immediately verify that the street or alley is indeed free of witnesses.(drone fly-throughs should have verified this beforehand) Document the exact location, including the street name and any notable landmarks, to ensure you can return to the same coordinates for your departure. It is crucial to have in your possession a timer linked to the exact timing of your arrival and planned departure. This device is essential for synchronizing with the precise timing of the return process (this protocol may vary depending on the technology used). The timer must match the exact moment the return loop comes around, ensuring a seamless and successful exit.

Rules of Manners for a Time Traveler in 1830s New Orleans

The following rules may not be relevant if you choose to minimize or entirely avoid interactions with the local population of the 1830s. For some visitors, the cultural and societal differences of the Antebellum South may prove overwhelming. The deeply ingrained social hierarchies, combined with the pervasive and unsettling reliance on enslaved labor and indentured servitude, can make engagement with the period both emotionally taxing and morally challenging.

For those who find these practices distressing, it may be preferable to observe the era from more of a distance, limiting direct involvement in its social customs. The widespread use of servants of whom are bound to their roles through coercion or outright ownership—underscores the stark and uncomfortable realities of this time. This system not only enforces rigid class distinctions but also places human suffering at the very foundation of daily life, a reality that modern visitors may find particularly difficult to reconcile with their values.

By choosing to minimize interaction, you can focus on observing the broader context of the period without becoming enmeshed in its more troubling aspects. However, if you do choose to engage with locals, it is important to approach these interactions with caution and sensitivity, keeping in mind the cultural norms and deeply ingrained systems of inequality that define 1830s New Orleans.

Planning Visits:

1. **Timing is Key**: Morning visits are friendly; afternoon visits are formal. Avoid visiting during meals or late evenings.
2. **Keep It Brief**: Ceremonial visits should last no longer than

15 minutes. Lingering is impolite, especially if others arrive.

Appearance:

1. **Dress Appropriately**: Formal visits require clean, polished attire; informal visits allow for simpler clothing.
2. **Be Groomed**: Ensure you are presentable; visible illness is unsuitable for formal visits.

Behavior During Visits:

1. **Seating Protocol**: Wait to be invited to sit. Offer the best seats to ladies or elders.
2. **Polite Posture**: Sit upright and avoid fidgeting or casual behavior.
3. **Defer to Rank**: Respect the social hierarchy in all interactions, prioritizing elders and those of higher status.

Conversational Etiquette:

1. **Speak Moderately**: Avoid loud, fast, or overly personal conversations.
2. **Be Observant**: If interrupted by letters or other visitors, suggest your host attend to them and prepare to leave.

Exiting Gracefully:

1. **Leave Quietly**: If others arrive, excuse yourself courteously. Avoid excessive goodbyes.
2. **Reciprocate Visits**: Formal visits must be returned within an appropriate timeframe.

Adapting to New Orleans:

Adapt to Local Customs: New Orleans in the 1830s is a unique blend of Creole, French, and Anglo-American influences. Understanding and embracing these cultural nuances will help you navigate its intricate social landscape. Observe local traditions and adjust your behavior accordingly to avoid standing out unnecessarily.

• • • •

Important Warning!! Navigating Interactions with Household Servants:

The role of servants in the Antebellum South is deeply intertwined with the rigid social hierarchy of the time. Unlike modern employees, virtually all servants are enslaved individuals or, bound to their roles through coercion, ownership, or economic necessity. Their lives are fraught with severe restrictions, constant surveillance, and limited autonomy. Interactions with these individuals must be approached with the utmost care and sensitivity.

As a time traveler, it is critical to respect the precarious position of household staff. Do not question their explanations about a host's availability, as such actions may create discomfort or even place them in jeopardy. Avoid any behavior that might draw undue attention to their actions or put them at risk of reprimand. Even seemingly minor requests, such as pressing for access to an unavailable host or assigning trivial tasks, could lead to significant consequences for the staff.

In this era, the treatment of servants—particularly enslaved individuals—was often harsh and unforgiving. Owners frequently enforced strict and punitive measures for even perceived infractions. A single misstep or misunderstanding on your part could result in severe punishment for the staff, making it vital to remain mindful of the fragile and unjust conditions under which they live.

When interacting with household staff, keep your engagement brief and polite. Refrain from unnecessary requests and maintain a respectful demeanor at all times. Always prioritize their well-being over convenience or curiosity, recognizing the immense challenges they face daily.

By showing empathy, discretion, and an awareness of these harsh realities, you can navigate this aspect of Antebellum New Orleans society with some degree of integrity. Let a sense of humanity guide your actions, ensuring that your presence does not contribute to the burdens already borne by those at the lowest rungs of this deeply stratified and unjust system.

Slavery and Free People of Color 1830s New Orleans

Considering the time and destination for this temporal travelers' guide, it deserves a worthy mention of the subject of slavery in antebellum New Orleans.

Slavery in 1830s New Orleans: A Critical Consideration for Temporal Travelers:

When traveling to 1830s New Orleans, it is imperative to understand the deeply entrenched system of slavery that underpins the city's social and economic fabric. At this time, New Orleans serves as the largest slave market in the United States, facilitating the purchase and sale of over 135,000 enslaved individuals. Approximately one in every three residents of the city is enslaved, underscoring the pervasive and all-encompassing nature of this institution.

Slave Pens and Auction Houses:

Enslaved people are often held in cramped and inhumane conditions within slave pens—secure, fenced areas where individuals are kept before being sold. These pens are typically located near major commercial hubs, such as the levee and bustling wharves, to facilitate easy access for traders and buyers. One of the most prominent locations for slave auctions is Hewlett's Exchange, a central venue where daily auctions take place, except on Sundays. Here, enslaved individuals are subjected to public inspections, where their physical condition and abilities are scrutinized to determine their market value. The process is profoundly dehumanizing, as families are frequently separated, and individuals are reduced to mere commodities.

The Mechanics of the Slave Trade:

The internal slave trade is a lucrative business, with traders like Isaac Franklin playing significant roles. Franklin and his partner John Armfield operate one of the most successful slave trading firms, handling hundreds of transactions annually. Enslaved individuals are meticulously cataloged, with detailed manifests listing their names, ages, physical descriptions, and any distinguishing marks. These records are essential for ensuring legal compliance following the 1808 federal ban on the importation of slaves from abroad. However, enforcement is lax, and domestic trading thrives, often driven by the high demand from sugar plantations and other labor-intensive industries in Louisiana.

Free People of Color:

In addition to the enslaved population, New Orleans is home to a substantial community of free people of color. These individuals occupy a unique and precarious position within society. While they enjoy certain freedoms and can own property, their status is continually threatened by pervasive racial prejudices and legal restrictions. Free people of color often serve as intermediaries in the slave trade, sometimes acting as agents or brokers. However, they also face significant discrimination and are subject to strict regulations that limit their rights and social mobility.

Navigating the Complexities:

For temporal travelers, navigating the realities of slavery in 1830s New Orleans requires a heightened awareness of the ethical and moral implications. Engaging with or inadvertently witnessing slave transactions can place one in morally compromising and legally precarious situations. Understanding the layout of slave pens, recognizing the signs of auction activities, and being aware of the presence of free people of color are essential for maintaining personal safety and ethical integrity. Additionally, temporal travelers should be mindful of the societal norms and legal frameworks that enforced and perpetuated slavery, ensuring respectful and informed interactions within this historical context.

By comprehensively understanding the brutal realities of slavery in 1830s New Orleans, temporal travelers can better prepare themselves to navigate the complexities of this era, fostering a deeper appreciation of the historical injustices that shaped the city's legacy.

Caution With Conveying Present-Day Prejudices:

As a visitor from a distant future, it is only natural to feel an instinctual urge to convey or advocate for your present-day values, prejudices, and attitudes regarding the injustices and horrors of slavery. However, it must be understood that you are merely a guest in the cruel reality of the Antebellum South—a world governed by norms and systems far removed from the ethical frameworks of your own time.

Caution and restraint must be exercised at all times. This is not to suggest that you must alter your emotions or suppress your moral stance on the abhorrent practice of slavery. Instead, it means you will be compelled to bury these feelings deep within yourself, as openly challenging the entrenched ideologies of this era could place you in grave danger or render you incapable of fulfilling your role as an observer.

The Antebellum South is not a place where modern notions of heroism can flourish. Here, you are an anonymous traveler, a silent witness to a world long consigned to the annals of history. Attempting to intervene or reshape this past would not only be futile but could disrupt the delicate balance of your journey, possibly endangering both yourself and the historical fabric you are observing.

While it may be agonizing to remain passive in the face of such glaring injustice, your presence in this time is not one of action but of reflection. Your task is to absorb, understand, and bear witness to the complexities and cruelties of this era. By doing so, you carry the lessons of this painful chapter back to your own time, where they may inform and inspire efforts to ensure that such horrors are never repeated.

This journey is not for the faint of heart. It demands a profound strength of will to endure the dissonance between your convictions and the grim reality surrounding you. Yet, in embracing this role of silent observer, you honor the memory of those who suffered and ensure their stories are not forgotten, even as you remain an unseen figure in a world that has long since vanished.

Appearances and Local Dress

As in 1930s Las Vegas, dressing to align with the local population is crucial for any temporal explorer. However, when venturing into the 1830s, this need becomes even more pronounced due to the stark differences in clothing styles and societal expectations. Proper attire not only helps you blend in but also ensures smoother interactions within a society where appearance often signals one's social standing.

The fashion of 1830s America is vastly different from contemporary styles, making it essential for any would-be traveler to arrive with at least one outfit that can pass as acceptable for the period. This initial attire will suffice for a short time—perhaps a day or two—but it is imperative to visit a tailor shop of the era as soon as possible to be fitted for clothing that aligns with the local norms. Authenticity in dress is not merely a matter of aesthetics; it is a practical tool for avoiding suspicion and unpleasant engagements.

When selecting your attire, consider the class and societal role of the individuals you intend to interact with. In Antebellum New Orleans, a deeply hierarchical society, clothing is a significant indicator of one's place in the social order. Whether you plan to move among the elite planter class, the burgeoning merchant community, or the working class, your appearance should reflect the conventions of the group you aim to engage with. Failure to do so could lead to misunderstandings or, worse, outright alienation.

For men, this might mean acquiring tailored suits, waistcoats, and appropriate hats reflective of their assumed status. For women, period-appropriate dresses, petticoats, bonnets, and gloves are essential to align with the expectations of femininity and modesty of the time. Accessories, such as walking sticks, pocket watches, or parasols, may also be necessary depending on the role you wish to portray.

In Antebellum New Orleans, where societal divisions are both pronounced and rigidly enforced, attention to clothing goes beyond vanity. It is a practical means of navigating the complex social fabric, signaling respect for local customs, and ensuring smoother interactions with its people. Whether you plan to blend into the bustling streets of the French Quarter, attend a formal gathering, or engage in more covert exploration, dressing appropriately will not only aid in your integration but also demonstrate your understanding of the time's cultural nuances.

By approaching this aspect of your journey with care and preparation, you will find that your attire becomes an essential tool for survival and success in the vibrant yet stratified world of the 1830s.

When planning for your arrival in the 1830s, it is crucial to secure appropriate clothing to help you blend seamlessly into the era's social fabric. Begin your preparations by researching costume shops in your area that specialize in period attire. Many such establishments carry historically inspired garments that could serve as a passable outfit for your initial days in the past. Additionally, consider reaching out to local theaters, community playhouses, or organizations that produce historical reenactments or performances. These venues often have access to costumes reflective of different time periods, and they may offer garments for sale, rent, or custom creation.

If costume shops or theaters are unavailable, online retailers that cater to historical enthusiasts or reenactors may provide suitable alternatives. However, be cautious about the accuracy of the clothing, as modern reproductions can sometimes miss the finer details that distinguish authentic 1830s attire. Pay close attention to materials, patterns, and construction to ensure your choice closely resembles what would have been worn during the era.

Once you have procured clothing that is reasonably suitable, remember that this will only serve as a temporary solution. Upon arriving in the 1830s, make it a priority to visit a tailor or dressmaker of the time to be fitted for attire that perfectly aligns with the local styles and expectations. This step is particularly important if you plan to interact with members of the local population, as poorly tailored or anachronistic clothing could draw unwanted attention or raise suspicion.

Preparing your wardrobe with care not only enhances your ability to blend in but also signals respect for the customs and societal norms of the era. Clothing is not just a practical consideration; it is a vital tool for navigating the intricate social hierarchies of the Antebellum South, allowing you to move through its world with greater ease and authenticity.

Important Advisory!!

Please bear in mind that depending on the particular century from which you are traveling to any distant past, maintaining discretion is paramount. Not only is it essential to remain undercover and anonymous while in the target year, but it is equally important to exercise caution and confidentiality when discussing your ventures with those you interact with in your present. This is especially true if time travel has not yet been widely recognized or accepted as a legitimate means of travel in your respective era.

In the 21st century, for instance, time travel is largely dismissed as theoretical or purely science fiction. Casually revealing your plans to venture into the annals of history would likely be met with skepticism or disbelief. Moreover, such disclosures could jeopardize your anonymity or lead to complications that might interfere with your temporal journey. It is wise to limit knowledge of your mission to only the most trusted individuals, if anyone at all.

If you are from a more distant future where time travel has become an accepted practice or even a commonplace activity, this advisory may not apply. However, for travelers from a period where temporal relocation remains speculative or highly classified, maintaining confidentiality is absolutely vital. Loose talk could risk exposing not only your plans but also the very existence of time travel, potentially altering the fabric of history or drawing unwanted attention to your activities.

Discretion is not just a matter of personal safety—it is a necessary safeguard to preserve the integrity of your mission and avoid unintended consequences. Regardless of your origin century, a cautious and judicious approach to sharing information about your journey will ensure that your temporal adventures remain successful, secure, and undisturbed by unnecessary interference.

Common Phrases in Early 1800s America:

Here are some expressions and terms that may have been commonly heard in the early 19th century. Bear in mind that local colloquialisms could vary considerably and that some of these phrases might not be exact for 1838-1839.

1. **"By and by"** – Soon or eventually.
2. **"Top of the morning"** – A cheerful greeting (more common in Irish communities).
3. **"A penny for your thoughts"** – Asking someone to share what they are thinking.
4. **"As the crow flies"** – A straight, direct route.
5. **"Don't cry over spilled milk"** – Don't lament what's already happened.
6. **"Make hay while the sun shines"** – Take advantage of opportunities while they last.
7. **"God willing and the creek don't rise"** – If nothing unforeseen prevents it.
8. **"Fixing to"** – Preparing to do something (common in Southern regions).
9. **"Devil of a time"** – A difficult experience.
10. **"I swan"** – An expression of surprise or disbelief (common in rural areas).

11. **"What in tarnation?"** – An exclamation of surprise or shock.
12. **"Highfalutin"** – Pretentious or overly fancy.
13. **"Knock into a cocked hat"** – To thoroughly defeat or surpass.

Early 19th-Century Accents and Pronunciation:

The accents and pronunciation of early American English varied greatly by region and were influenced by the diverse origins of settlers.

1. **Southern Dialects**: In New Orleans, the Southern drawl was influenced by French, Spanish, and Creole languages, giving the speech a melodic quality. Words borrowed from French often retained a distinctive pronunciation, like "Creole" ([kree-ohl]) and "Lagniappe" ([lan-yap], meaning a little extra).
2. **New England Accents**: Coastal accents in the North often dropped the "r" sound in words like "car" (pronounced *cah*) or "farm" (*fahm*).
3. **Frontier Speech**: In rural or less settled areas, speech was often slower, with strong influences from Irish and Scottish immigrants. This included terms like "reckon" (to think or suppose) and "ain't" (a contraction for "am not" or "is not").

The Cultural Melting Pot of 1830s New Orleans:

1830s New Orleans was a vibrant and diverse city, shaped by French, Spanish, African, Caribbean, and Anglo-American influences. The city was a hub of commerce, culture, and immigration, resulting in a unique Creole identity. This melting pot gave rise to a rich tapestry of languages, including French, Spanish, Creole, and English, as well as diverse traditions in music, cuisine, and social practices.

The local dialect often blended French and African influences, with Creole being widely spoken in the city. French phrases like "bonjour" (good day) and "merci" (thank you) were common, as were terms like "voodoo" and "gumbo," which reflected the cultural fusion.

Advice for Temporal Explorers:

1. **Learn Key Phrases**: Familiarize yourself with both formal English of the time and common colloquialisms, especially if you plan to interact with locals. Knowing phrases like "I reckon" or "fixing to" can help you blend in with rural and Southern communities.
2. **Adapt to Local Speech**: Listen carefully to regional accents and try to mirror them subtly to avoid standing out. In New Orleans, understanding basic French words and Creole terms can make a significant difference in social interactions in some cases.
3. **Understand Social Hierarchies**: Be aware of the deep societal divides in Antebellum New Orleans. Class distinctions, linguistic differences, and cultural nuances will shape your interactions.

Treading Lightly: The Risks of Bringing Technology to 1830s New Orleans

When considering bringing modern gadgets to 1830s New Orleans, temporal travelers must exercise great care in both protecting their devices and ensuring they remain undetected by the locals. The 19th century presents a vastly different world where advanced technology would be viewed as completely alien, potentially provoking fear, suspicion, or even hostility. This makes discretion, planning, and protective measures absolutely essential.

Modern devices, such as smartphones, tablets, or e-readers, are invaluable tools for storing information like historical maps, cultural notes, or even period newspapers such as The Orleans Bee and The True American. These files can provide critical insights into the local social, political, and economic environment, allowing travelers to blend in more effectively and understand the events of the time. However, these devices are not designed to withstand the environmental challenges of the 1830s, particularly in a city like New Orleans, known for its high humidity, frequent rainfall, and generally unpredictable weather.

Protecting Your Gadgets:

1. **Waterproof and Dustproof Cases**: Equip your devices with protective cases to shield them from moisture, dust, and accidental damage.
2. **Solar Chargers**: Since electricity is non-existent in this time period, solar chargers are essential for powering your gadgets. These portable chargers will allow you to harness sunlight to keep your devices operational.
3. **Periodic Maintenance**: Take time to clean and check your

devices for any signs of damage caused by the challenging environment.

Maintaining Discretion:

The importance of keeping modern gadgets hidden from the local population cannot be overstated. In 1830s New Orleans, such devices would be entirely incomprehensible to the locals and could lead to alarm, suspicion, or even accusations of sorcery. To avoid these risks:

- **Use Concealable Storage**: Carry gadgets in inconspicuous, period-appropriate bags or containers that do not draw attention.

- **Operate in Private**: Use your devices only in secure, isolated locations where there is no chance of being observed by others.

- **Prevent Unauthorized Access**: Ensure devices are locked with passwords or other secure measures to prevent misuse if accidentally discovered. Though, this precaution is probably not necessary, considering the time period.

Purposeful Usage:

Your devices should serve specific, mission-critical functions, and loading them with historical documents, such as digitized versions of *The Orleans Bee* or *The True American*, is a highly practical use. These newspapers provide valuable context about local events, political climates, and cultural nuances, offering a direct window into the daily life and mindset of 1830s New Orleans. They also contain practical details like racing results from the Eclipse and Metairie racetracks, which were major social and sporting events of the time, as well as lottery results from various locations across the city, reflecting the city's fascination with games of chance. Knowing these results will aid in mitigating the challenges of procuring local currency in 1830s New Orleans. Additionally, these newspapers offer a wealth of advertisements showcasing proprietors selling everything from food items, salted meats, ales, wines, and other local goods that may be required or sought after during your stay.

In book three, **Las Vegas Revisited**, Will gives account of his and Charle's visit to the Bishop's Hotel in New Orleans....*We won again! The total amount came to $9,900, as some smaller prizes were awarded from the same $10,000 pot. Yesterday, we arrived at Bishop's Hotel, headed to the cafe for a beer, and then patiently waited. At precisely 5 PM, amidst a lot of fanfare, extravagance, and a multitude of announcements, they commenced drawing the numbers for that day's lottery. The ticket class was "64," which happened was the exact class of the two tickets we purchased the day before. We had all 12 numbers that were drawn yesterday. I suppose we're pretty lucky?! The payments are made immediately once you present the winning ticket, in fact, they try to capitalize on the occasional winner, afterall, that's what attracts more players"!*

Avoiding Exposure: (Reiterated earlier, as the importance of this measure can't be stressed enough)

To prevent accidental discovery or suspicion:

- **Minimize Public Usage**: Refrain from using gadgets in open spaces or situations where others might notice.

- **Prepare for Emergencies**: Have a contingency plan for securing or disabling your devices if there is a risk of exposure.

- **Blend with the Era**: Familiarize yourself with local customs and behaviors to avoid attracting attention, even if your gadgets remain hidden.

By taking these precautions and using your devices thoughtfully, you can enhance your temporal experience without jeopardizing your mission or disrupting the historical timeline. Always prioritize the integrity of the era and your own safety, ensuring that your modern tools remain valuable assets rather than potential liabilities.

Reminder:

Since solar chargers are the only way to power your smartphones, tablets, or other devices, it is essential to ensure that, when checking in at a hotel or guest house, your window faces a direction where sunlight can adequately reach your room or apartment.

· · · · ·

Regarding Other Items From Your Respective Time:

As mentioned in the previous *Las Vegas Revealed* guide, any items or articles from your time will stand out as conspicuously foreign in 1830s New Orleans. Everyday items such as shampoo bottles, deodorant containers, medicines, and other modern conveniences will appear utterly alien and incomprehensible to an observer from this era. Their unfamiliarity could provoke anything from suspicion to fear, potentially compromising your anonymity or safety.

It cannot be overstated how critical it is to keep such items hidden at all times, especially from maids, cleaning staff, or servants who may enter your room for routine tidying. These individuals are accustomed to their time's specific objects and routines, and any exposure to unfamiliar items could lead to unwanted attention or questions. Even innocent curiosity could result in your belongings being discussed among others, increasing the risk of discovery.

After using any item, it is imperative to immediately pack it away securely in your backpack or a designated safe spot. Choose a place that is inconspicuous and not easily accessed by others. Avoid leaving items in open view, even briefly, and consider using period-appropriate luggage or containers to further camouflage your belongings.

By taking these precautions, you can maintain the confidentiality of your temporal journey and ensure that your modern-day items do not disrupt the historical setting or draw undue attention from the people of 1830s New Orleans. Remember, discretion is key to your success as a temporal visitor.

Temporal Sickness- Understanding and Managing Side Effects of Time Travel:

For temporal visitors, managing health during time travel involves addressing a unique concern: **temporal sickness**. However, advancements in temporal displacement technology may prevent this condition for some visitors entirely. Those fortunate enough to use advanced methods that stabilize temporal energy fields are unlikely to experience any discomfort. For others, especially those utilizing less advanced techniques, understanding and mitigating temporal sickness is crucial.

Understanding Temporal Sickness:

Temporal sickness, akin to severe motion sickness, occurs when the strain of passing through temporal distortion fields disrupts the traveler's physiology. Symptoms may include **nausea, dizziness, headaches, and occasional vomiting**, leading to feelings of disorientation. These effects are thought to result from the interaction between the traveler's nervous system and the temporal energies encountered during transit. While the exact mechanisms remain unclear, the rapid shift between temporal coordinates appears to place stress on the body, similar to the effects of extreme motion or pressure changes.

Precautions and Management for Those Affected:

For travelers at risk of temporal sickness, the following precautions can help manage symptoms:

- **Stay Indoors**: Rest in a stable and controlled environment, such as your hotel room, to minimize exposure to external stimuli that may worsen symptoms.

- **Hydrate and Nourish**: Drink plenty of water(if possible) and consume light, easily digestible foods to support your body's recovery. Avoid alcohol and heavy meals, which can exacerbate nausea.

- **Limit Movement**: Avoid excessive movement or strenuous activities. Resting in a reclined or seated position can help reduce dizziness and disorientation.

- **Use Remedies**: Over-the-counter medications for motion sickness, such as **dimenhydrinate** or **meclizine**, can provide temporary relief. Consult with a healthcare provider familiar with temporal travel for tailored recommendations.(Assuming there are those familiar or aware or temporal displacement in your respective time)

- **Practice Relaxation**: Stress and anxiety can amplify symptoms. Deep breathing, meditation, or listening to calming music may help maintain a sense of equilibrium.

Most symptoms subside within 48 hours, allowing the traveler to resume activities without lingering effects. In rare cases, where symptoms persist, seeking temporal medical assistance is advisable after your return to your respective time.

For Those Without Symptoms:

If your temporal displacement method prevents temporal sickness, these precautions are unnecessary. You can enjoy your visit without interruption, though vigilance regarding other health risks of the

1830s—such as diseases and environmental hazards—remains essential. For all visitors, preparation and awareness are the keys to a safe and enjoyable temporal journey.

With proper planning, even those prone to temporal sickness can recover quickly and fully immerse themselves in the historical wonders of their destination.

The following serves as a comprehensive guide for any temporal traveler venturing to 1830s New Orleans. Given the constraints of packing and the limited space available for bringing essential items, it is imperative to choose your supplies wisely. Your selection should be based on the anticipated length of your stay, the nature of your activities, and the capacity in which you will be exploring and navigating this unique time and place.

New Orleans in the 1830s is a bustling, vibrant city steeped in history, but it is also a locale fraught with the health risks and environmental challenges characteristic of the Antebellum South. From its humid subtropical climate, which fosters the proliferation of disease-carrying mosquitoes, to its rampant unsanitary urban conditions, your journey will require careful preparation. Whether you are a historian, adventurer, or scientific observer, your ability to thrive—and survive—in this era hinges on thoughtful planning and preparation.

Advisory for Maintaining Good Health in the Antebellum South:

As a time traveler visiting the Antebellum South in the 1830s, you must take proactive steps to protect your health in an era lacking modern medical knowledge and treatments. Here are some specific recommendations:

1. Hygiene and Sanitation

- **Water Safety:** Always boil water before consuming it to eliminate waterborne pathogens that cause diseases like typhoid fever and dysentery.(in 1830s New Orleans this can't be stressed enough)

- **Food Precautions:** Avoid uncooked or poorly cooked food. Stick to meals prepared under your supervision when possible.

- **Personal Hygiene:** Regular handwashing with soap (Bring a modern antibacterial soap) is essential, especially before eating and after any exposure to public areas.

2. Preventing Mosquito-Borne Illnesses

- **Clothing:** Wear long-sleeved shirts, long pants, and hats to minimize mosquito bites.(period appropriate)

- **Insect Repellent:** Bring a modern, DEET-based insect repellent for effective protection.

- **Mosquito Nets:** Sleep under treated mosquito nets to prevent malaria and yellow fever.

3. Vaccinations

- **Smallpox:** Ensure you are vaccinated before traveling. This was a major killer but preventable with prior inoculation.

- **Typhoid Fever and Measles:** Get modern vaccines to reduce your risk of these illnesses.

- **Yellow Fever Vaccine:** While it doesn't cure the disease, it offers effective prevention.

Essential Remedies and Supplies for a Time Traveler:

Modern medicine has made many deadly 19th-century diseases manageable. Bring the following with you to protect yourself or to assist others:

Antibiotics

- **Broad-Spectrum Antibiotics (e.g., Amoxicillin, Doxycycline):** Useful for treating bacterial infections like typhoid fever and secondary infections resulting from diseases like dysentery.

- **Metronidazole:** Effective against parasitic causes of dysentery.

• • • •

Antimalarial Medications

- **Quinine or Modern Alternatives (e.g., Malarone, Doxycycline):** Carry these to both prevent and treat malaria.

- **Artemisinin Combination Therapies (ACTs):** Effective in treating severe malaria.

Antivirals and Vaccines

- While effective antivirals may be unavailable from your century, for historical diseases like smallpox and measles, undergo modern immunizations and supportive treatments like antipyretics (fever reducers).

Symptom Management

- **Pain Relievers/Fever Reducers:** Bring acetaminophen or ibuprofen to alleviate fever and body aches.

- **Oral Rehydration Salts (ORS):** Crucial for treating dehydration from dysentery or cholera-like illnesses.

- **Antidiarrheal Medications:** Use cautiously to manage severe diarrhea (e.g., loperamide).

Sterilization and Wound Care

- **Alcohol or Iodine Swabs:** For disinfecting cuts and abrasions to prevent infections.

- **Bandages and Sterile Dressings:** Carry a robust supply for wound care.

Other Supplies

- **Activated Charcoal:** Useful for treating some cases of poisoning or gastrointestinal distress.

- **Modern Antiseptics:** Bring povidone-iodine or hydrogen peroxide.

- **First Aid Manual:** Tailored for low-resource environments with simple, clear instructions.

General Precautions

- **Avoid Crowds and Epidemic Zones:** Stay away from areas with known outbreaks of diseases like yellow fever or smallpox.

- **Minimize Contact:** Avoid direct interaction with visibly ill individuals.

- **Medical Assistance:** If engaging with local populations, offer your remedies cautiously, as they may be skeptical of foreign practices. This issue is fraught with concern, as administering modern-day remedies to locals may violate certain protocols or risk exposing your true origins. Extreme discretion is advised in this matter.

These measures can significantly mitigate the risks of disease and infection while you navigate the health challenges of the Antebellum South.

<u>*Important Note:*</u>

Another important consideration for the temporal explorer is the choice of accommodations. In a region and time so far removed from the modern world, it is crucial to make every effort to stay in one of the higher-class hotels of 1830s New Orleans and to avoid lodgings of a more local or rustic character, where hygiene is likely to be severely lacking. Although sterilization practices and antiseptic cleaning products do not exist in this era, higher-class accommodations will provide a relatively safer environment by removing you from the squalor and unsanitary conditions that plague many parts of the city.

Opting for an upscale hotel offers not only a measure of protection from infectious diseases but also the convenience and comfort of a private residence. These establishments often feature better-maintained living spaces and access to rudimentary amenities that allow for personal preventive measures. For instance, you can wipe down surfaces in your room with modern sanitizing materials you bring along, ensuring a cleaner and safer environment. Additionally, access to private bathing facilities—something rarely available...period.—will enable you to maintain personal hygiene more effectively.

The privacy and resources of these higher-class accommodations also empower you to implement other precautionary measures. You can safely store your supplies, avoid direct contact with potentially contaminated communal spaces, and control your exposure to environments where diseases such as typhoid, dysentery, or malaria are more likely to spread. While these measures cannot eliminate all risks, they significantly reduce the likelihood of contracting a serious illness during your stay in this historically fascinating yet challenging time and place.

Money and Finances

As addressed in the previous guide, *Las Vegas Revealed*, acquiring currency from the 1830s will be both even more challenging and expensive for any modern-day temporal traveler. Coins, often referred to as "specie" during that era, are particularly costly to obtain from coin shops or antique dealers due to their rarity and historical value. Despite the expense, obtaining an adequate supply of authentic 1830s currency—either in coin or banknote form—is an unavoidable necessity before embarking on any mission to this time period.

Banknotes present additional complications. In the 1830s, paper currency was issued not by a centralized government, but by individual banks scattered across the country. These banknotes varied significantly in design, quality, and acceptance. A note issued by one bank might be refused entirely in another part of the country, making them an unreliable means of exchange in unfamiliar regions. Furthermore, certain banks had a stronger reputation for stability, meaning their notes were more widely accepted. Acquiring these "preferred" banknotes can be a time-consuming and labor-intensive process, requiring careful research and planning.

Adding to the complexity is the historical context of the 1830s financial system. The period was marked by economic instability, culminating in the Panic of 1837, a financial crisis that spiraled into a six-year depression with profound and lasting effects on the American economy. This crisis—essentially a mini-depression—further eroded public confidence in banknotes, making their acceptance even more precarious. Travelers relying solely on paper currency during this time may face significant challenges, as the value and trustworthiness of such notes could vary greatly by region and issuing institution.

The Panic of 1837 had broader repercussions than immediate financial instability. Domestically, it spurred innovations in how business credit was assessed. In response to the economic collapse and the resulting wave of business failures, Lewis Tappan—a prominent abolitionist and entrepreneur—founded the Mercantile Agency in 1841. This organization collected and shared credit information about businesses across the country, creating one of the first systematic efforts to evaluate financial trustworthiness. Drawing on a national network of correspondents, Tappan's firm laid the foundation for the modern credit reporting industry, which remains a cornerstone of financial infrastructure today, primarily as a commercial enterprise rather than a social reform initiative.

The effects of the crisis also rippled across the globe, particularly impacting trade with China. In the years leading up to the Panic, rapid credit expansion fueled speculation in tea, silk, and other luxury goods from the Celestial Empire. When the bubble burst, merchant houses from London to New York and Boston suffered catastrophic failures. This downturn significantly altered global trade dynamics. For instance, many New England traders, such as J.P. Cushing, redirected their capital away from the volatile China trade and into burgeoning domestic industries like American railroads. This shift marked a pivotal moment in the economic realignment of American capital, spurring industrial growth and infrastructure development in the United States.

The interconnectedness of these events underscores the complexities of navigating the financial landscape of the 1830s. For temporal travelers, understanding these historical underpinnings is vital to managing resources effectively and avoiding pitfalls in an era of economic uncertainty.

Given these difficulties, it is strongly advised to bring as much coins possible and carefully selected banknotes. Coins, while heavier and more cumbersome, were universally accepted and held intrinsic value, serving as a reliable backup in areas where banknotes might be refused.

In Book Three of Retrorsum, Las Vegas Revisited, both Will Patterson and Charles Damron employ an ingenious strategy to acquire money appropriate to the respective time period: they play various lotteries. The first lottery they play in takes place in Richmond, Virginia, during their journey to New Orleans. Their success in the Richmond lottery is no accident—they possess winning numbers sourced from a historical Richmond newspaper of the era, providing them with a distinct advantage. This calculated approach allows them to obtain funds without arousing suspicion, ensuring their ability to blend seamlessly into their surroundings.

Similarly, upon arriving in New Orleans, Will and Charles repleated their strategy by entering another local lottery. This time, their focus is on acquiring currency specific to the New Orleans area, a crucial move in a time when regional banknotes were not always interchangeable or widely accepted in different parts of the country. Winning the lottery in New Orleans provides them with the local currency they need to navigate the city's economic landscape, facilitating their endeavors without the complications of dealing with unfamiliar or unaccepted forms of money.

The decision to win currency through lotteries proves to be a remarkably advantageous tactic for temporal travelers. Not only does it provide them with legitimate, locally recognized funds, but it also allows them to sidestep the challenges associated with purchasing large amounts of 1830s currency in the present. Additionally, by utilizing historical records to identify winning numbers, they minimize the risk of detection, ensuring that their actions remain consistent with the temporal norms of their surroundings.

Another advantage was that the winnings were more than generous for the time, enabling both Will and Charles to take up residence at the St. Charles Hotel, which, as mentioned earlier, would be the optimal choice for any "future" visitors to the city.

The coinage of the 1830s offers a fascinating glimpse into the monetary system of the era, and for the temporal visitor, it will be both strange and exciting to hold and examine these unique pieces while exploring daily life. Among the coins in circulation, you will find:

• *Half-Cent Pieces:* These small copper coins, worth half a cent, are a rarity by modern standards and were already being phased out by the mid-19th century.

• *Large Cents:* Much larger than today's pennies, these copper coins are roughly the size of a modern quarter and carry intricate designs that reflect the artistry of the time.

• *Half Dimes:* Predating the modern nickel, these tiny silver coins are worth five cents and are some of the smallest coins in U.S. history, both in size and weight.

• *Bust Quarters and Seated Quarters:* Silver coins worth 25 cents, these two designs dominated the era. Bust quarters feature the profile of Liberty in a classical style, while seated quarters depict Liberty seated with a shield, symbolizing strength and protection.

• *Bust Dollars and Half Dollars:* Larger silver coins, worth one and half a dollar respectively, these were widely used for significant transactions and boast elaborate designs that make them prized among numismatists.

• *Gold Pieces of Various Denominations:* Gold coinage, such as quarter eagles (worth $2.50), half eagles ($5), and eagles ($10), were highly valuable and mainly used for substantial transactions. Their gold content made them a tangible representation of wealth and security.

For the temporal visitor and coin enthusiasts alike, the 1830s is an unparalleled time to explore the evolution of American currency. Each coin not only serves as a means of exchange but also as a miniature piece of history, embodying the economic practices, artistic sensibilities, and craftsmanship of a bygone era. Handling these coins provides a tangible connection to the past, offering a unique opportunity to appreciate the monetary landscape of 19th-century America.

Important Note:

Before the local acquisition of 1830s currency can be established, it may be necessary to bring along some unmarked gold ingots or other precious items to trade, barter, or exchange for local currency. Gold was universally valued during this period, making it an ideal medium for such transactions. By offering gold in a form that lacks identifying marks or modern features, temporal travelers can ensure a smooth exchange without raising suspicion. Precious metals like gold are not only universally accepted but also highly versatile, allowing for negotiations across different regions and economic contexts. This strategy provides a practical and secure way to acquire the necessary funds for navigating the financial landscape of the 1830s.

Emotional and Romantic Considerations for Temporal Visitors to Late 1830s New Orleans

For temporal visitors venturing to the vibrant yet deeply complex world of **1830s New Orleans**, the allure of forming emotional or romantic bonds with locals must be approached with the utmost caution. The disparity between your 21st-century perspective (or later century) and the cultural, social, and economic norms of the antebellum South is far greater than the difference between modern-day experiences and, for instance, the 1930s of Las Vegas. This vast gap may render genuine emotional connections difficult, if not impossible, to achieve on an equal footing. For many travelers, this cultural chasm proves too wide to bridge, leaving any notion of lasting emotional bonds fraught with potential misunderstandings, ethical dilemmas, and unintended consequences.

Understanding the Challenges of Emotional Bonding:

The antebellum South is a world shaped by stark societal hierarchies, rigid gender roles, and a deeply entrenched economic system reliant on slavery. These dynamics create interpersonal and cultural divides that a modern traveler may find insurmountable. While basic human needs—companionship, understanding, and love—remain constant across eras, the socio-economic structures, language, customs, and moral codes of the 1830s differ so significantly from modern norms that establishing a meaningful, equitable relationship with a local is exceedingly complex.

For example, emotional intimacy in this era is often constrained by strict societal expectations. Women, especially in the upper and middle classes, are bound by rigid domestic roles, while men face societal pressures to adhere to notions of honor and propriety. For those outside these classes, such as the marginalized or enslaved populations, emotional and social realities are dictated by systems of oppression and exploitation that starkly contrast with contemporary values.

For the temporal visitor, these disparities mean that any emotional bond risks being one-sided or based on a profound lack of mutual understanding. Moreover, even fleeting connections could lead to significant ethical and historical consequences. Just as **Will Patterson** discovered in *Retrorsum, Book One*, the desire for companionship in an alien time can press heavily upon you, tempting you to forge bonds that may distort not only your personal journey but the timeline itself.

Guidelines for Navigating Emotional Involvement in the Antebellum South:

1. Acknowledge the Cultural Divide

The social, economic, and racial inequalities of the 1830s are stark and may clash profoundly with your modern sensibilities. Recognize that these differences are not merely inconveniences but structural realities that define every aspect of interpersonal relationships in this era. Understanding this context is vital to interpreting the behavior, motivations, and expectations of locals without imposing your contemporary perspectives.

2. Be Aware of Emotional Misalignment

Your longing for companionship or connection may stem more from the isolation of time travel than from a true affinity for an individual.

Relationships formed under these circumstances risk being based on novelty or misunderstanding rather than genuine compatibility. Keep in mind that locals may perceive you as mysterious or exotic, which could influence their interactions with you in ways that do not reflect authentic emotional connection.

3. Avoid Deep Romantic Entanglements

Engaging in a romantic relationship carries significant risks, both emotionally and ethically. Given the vast cultural and historical divide, such a bond could inadvertently harm the individual involved by altering their life path or introducing them to concepts and emotions they might struggle to contextualize within their world. Additionally, any attachment you form may lead to the temptation to stay in the 1830s, with all the attendant complications of legal documentation, livelihood, and historical consequences.

4. Balance Empathy with Non-Interference

While it is natural to feel empathy for individuals living in this challenging era, remember that your role as a temporal visitor is primarily observational. Engaging too deeply risks not only altering individual lives but potentially destabilizing the historical continuum. Instead of seeking to "fix" perceived injustices or difficulties, focus on understanding the context in which these individuals live.

5. Maintain Emotional Boundaries

Set clear limits for your interactions. For example:

- Avoid discussions about future events or technologies.

- Refrain from offering advice that could influence significant decisions.
- Keep conversations neutral and grounded in the context of the time.

6. Mitigate Loneliness Through Preparation

Before traveling, establish strategies for coping with the isolation inherent to temporal displacement. Journaling, maintaining a sense of purpose, and focusing on your mission can help alleviate the emotional strain without requiring deep bonds with locals.

Having a generous collection of downloaded contemporary files, including music and even movies from your home time, can also help mitigate the effects of temporal isolation, especially during extended stays.

• • • •

7. Anticipate Ethical Dilemmas

Disclosing your true nature as a time traveler may spark disbelief, fear, or efforts to exploit your knowledge. Avoid revealing your origin or future insights, as this could irreparably disrupt the timeline. Adopt a cover story that aligns with the era's norms to explain any peculiarities in your behavior or speech. For any temporal visitor in the 1830s, this is paramount, being the disparity of differences between your time and the 1830s is extreme.

8. Document Your Experiences

Keep a record of your interactions and emotional responses. Reflecting on these experiences upon returning to your original time can help you process any feelings of attachment or regret while guiding future temporal journeys.

In *Book Three, Las Vegas Revisited*, Will Patterson wrote of his willingness to maintain a distance from the local population due to the extreme differences in thoughts, feelings, and prejudices of the time.

Final Thoughts for the Temporal Visitor:

While the allure of forming emotional or romantic bonds in 1830s New Orleans may be strong, the disparity between your perspective and the realities of this era is profound. Emotional entanglements, though seemingly comforting, carry risks not only to the individuals involved but to the historical fabric you are meant to preserve. By adhering to clear boundaries and focusing on your mission, you can navigate these challenges with empathy and integrity, ensuring that your temporal journey remains a respectful exploration rather than an intrusive alteration of the past.

Preparing for the Possibility of Being Stranded in 1830s New Orleans:

For temporal travelers to 1830s New Orleans, the possibility of being unable to return to the present is a real and daunting risk. Equipment malfunctions, environmental factors like storms, or missed departure coordinates could leave you stranded indefinitely. Preparing for such a scenario is essential to ensure survival and minimize disruption to the historical timeline.

Be advised that some of the following may or may not apply to you.

Key Preparations for Indefinite Survival:

1. Establish Multiple Exit Strategies

Identify alternative departure locations and ensure familiarity with the geography and transportation methods of the 1830s. Have backup plans for weather delays or other logistical disruptions that could hinder your ability to reach a designated site.

2. Secure and Encode Essential Data

Bring vital information about future events, economic trends, and historical sports outcomes. Store this data in two formats:

○ **Digital Archive**: Use a secure, password-protected device.

○ **Hard Copy Backup**: Encode notes using private shorthand or cryptic references to make them indecipherable to locals.

○ Remember, if you suspect that your gadgets may break or fail to function, be sure to write down vital information in paper form, such as in a journal. This will provide you with access to critical data in the event that your tablets, laptops, or smartphones no longer work.

3. This knowledge can be leveraged to generate income through strategic wagers or investments, ensuring financial stability in a time with limited employment opportunities.

4. Adapt to Local Conditions

Learn the basics of self-sufficiency, including foraging, navigation, and cultural norms. Adopting a plausible local identity will help you blend in and avoid unnecessary scrutiny. Choose a neutral cover story, such as a merchant or traveler, to deflect suspicion about your background.

5. Minimize Risk of Equipment Loss

Never carry the entirety of your archive when venturing into public spaces.(in paper form) Only take the information you need for specific activities,(write down on period appropriate stationary) leaving the primary records securely hidden.

6. Anticipate the Emotional Toll

Being stranded in the 1830s means confronting a world without modern conveniences, familiar social norms, or access to advanced medical care. Emotional resilience and flexibility will be critical to adapting to this reality.

Important Note!

Avoiding Pregnancy: For women travelers on long-term missions or in the event of becoming stranded in the distant past (such as the 1830s), avoiding pregnancy is vital for both practical and health-related reasons. Childbirth in the early 1800s is fraught with significant dangers, including high rates of maternal and infant mortality due to the lack of modern medical knowledge, sanitation, and emergency interventions. These risks can be life-threatening and should be carefully considered when planning for temporal travel.

It is essential to abstain from emotional entanglements or relationships that could lead to pregnancy. As an additional precaution, ensure you bring reliable birth control methods from your home time. These modern solutions offer a critical safeguard against unintended pregnancy in an era where such issues could become catastrophic. Proper preparation and adherence to these precautions will help minimize risks and ensure your mission remains focused and successful. (As mentioned in Las Vegas Revisited.)

• • • •

Further Advice for Temporal Travelers:

While no preparation can eliminate all risks, thorough planning can significantly increase your chances of surviving—and even thriving—in the 1830s should you become stranded. Knowledge, adaptability, and careful concealment of your origins will be your greatest assets in navigating this unfamiliar world indefinitely.

In *Book Three of Retrorsum: Las Vegas Revisited*, during the second attempt to bring Charles back to the present, Elizabeth and Charles choose to wait out their time not in New Orleans but in Savannah, Georgia. There, they befriend a local woman who owns a guesthouse, providing them with a stable base. During their stay, they learn to grow their own food and take meticulous precautions in cooking to ensure their safety. They avoid traveling to New Orleans until the precise window for their return to the present is set to occur. This strategic decision ultimately aids in their survival, ensuring they remain prepared and protected until the designated return date arrives.

Food and Drink

In the antebellum South, cuisine was a vibrant mosaic shaped by diverse cultural influences and the region's plentiful natural resources. Typical meals prominently featured a variety of **game meats** such as rabbit, squirrel, venison, bear, wild turkey, duck, pheasant, quail, and raccoon. These wild animals were not only a vital source of protein but also reflected the rural and frontier lifestyles of many Southerners. **Pork** remained a staple due to its versatility and the ease with which it could be raised, providing a reliable source of meat for both everyday meals and special occasions. Essential grains like **rice** and **corn** were fundamental to the Southern diet, commonly used in beloved dishes such as cornbread and gumbo. Coastal regions, particularly cities like New Orleans, saw a significant influence from French culinary traditions, leading to the prevalence of **seafood** such as catfish, shrimp, and crab in local cuisine.

The culinary practices of the antebellum South thus illustrate a complex interplay between available resources, cultural heritage, and the challenging realities of the time. The reliance on a wide array of game meats not only provided necessary sustenance but also connected Southerners to the land and their cultural roots. Meanwhile, the pervasive health challenges underscored the dire need for improved sanitation and public health measures. The diets of enslaved people, enriched by African culinary traditions, laid the groundwork for what would later evolve into the distinctive and beloved flavors of Southern soul food, highlighting the enduring legacy of this era's food culture.

Important Note: Slave Diet of the Antebellum South:

In the antebellum South, the diet of enslaved individuals was shaped by a combination of imposed rations and their own resourcefulness in *cultivating and foraging for additional sustenance. Enslaved people were typically provided with basic rations such as cornmeal or rice, which they had to process themselves by grinding or milling. These staples were often supplemented with small amounts of salted or smoked pork, not as a primary source of protein but rather as a means to add necessary salt to their meals. Beyond the rations, enslaved individuals cultivated their own gardens, growing vegetables like turnips, cabbage, peas, and snap beans, which provided essential nutrients and variety to their diet. They also hunted wild game such as rabbits, squirrels, and wild turkey, and foraged for fruits like watermelons to aid in hydration. For those who adhered to specific dietary restrictions, such as Muslim enslaved people who refused to consume pork, alternative rations like salt beef or fish were provided. Additionally, enslaved cooks played a crucial role in preparing meals, often incorporating African culinary traditions and utilizing available ingredients creatively to enhance their limited provisions. This combination of forced rations and self-sufficiency allowed enslaved individuals to sustain themselves despite the harsh conditions and limited resources imposed upon them, highlighting their resilience and ingenuity in maintaining their cultural and dietary practices under oppressive circumstances.*

<u>Advisory:</u>

For temporal visitors to 1830s New Orleans, exercising caution within the city's vibrant culinary scene is absolutely vital. Even during the 1830s, New Orleans offered a diverse array of dining options and eateries, ranging from upscale restaurants like in the St. Charles, the Verandah, and the St. Louis hotels to more modest local taverns. However, it is crucial to remain aware of the significant differences in food safety and hygiene practices compared to the modern era. Temptation may sometimes lead travelers to indulge in the appealing dishes of the time, potentially causing them to overlook the century they are visiting. While many offerings on paper sound delectable, maintaining vigilance is essential to avoid falling ill.

Cleanliness during the antebellum period was generally poor, with limited understanding of sanitation contributing to the spread of foodborne illnesses such as typhoid fever, cholera, and dysentery. Dysentery, for instance, was a prevalent and often deadly disease caused by bacteria or parasites found in contaminated food and water. Symptoms included bloody diarrhea, fever, nausea, and severe cramps. Treatments were largely ineffective and sometimes exacerbated the condition, as physicians commonly used purgatives like turpentine or castor oil, which only worsened the illness. The lack of proper sanitation in both urban and rural settings made diseases like dysentery a common and deadly threat, underscoring the importance of cautious dining practices.

To mitigate these health risks, temporal visitors should prioritize dining in reputable establishments known for better cleanliness and hygiene standards were apparently better than most. Avoiding street food vendors and ensuring that all consumed food is thoroughly cooked and properly stored can significantly reduce the likelihood of contracting illnesses.

*In **Book Three** of Retrorsum, Las Vegas Revisited, both Will and Charles frequently opted for **dried and cured meats and cheeses** as their primary sources of sustenance. They deliberately chose to dine in local eateries only rarely, even avoiding the restaurants located within the aforementioned high-end hotels. This cautious approach was driven by their awareness of the poor hygiene standards prevalent in many dining establishments of the antebellum South, which posed significant health risks such as foodborne illnesses like typhoid fever, cholera, and dysentery. By relying on preserved foods that were less susceptible to spoilage and contamination, Will and Charles were able to mitigate the risk of falling ill while navigating the complex and often perilous culinary landscape of 1830s New Orleans. Additionally, their preference for dried and cured products allowed them greater control over their diet, ensuring the quality* *and safety of the foods they consumed in an era where sanitation practices were rudimentary at best. This strategic choice not only safeguarded their health but also provided them with the flexibility to sustain themselves without depending heavily on the unreliable and often unsafe local food establishments.*

Purchasing Food Items from Ship Arrivals in the Port Area:

In **Book Three** of *Retrorsum, Las Vegas Revisited,* Will and Charles strategically sourced their sustenance by frequently purchasing food items from local shops and the bustling shipyards along the New Orleans waterfront. They particularly favored **cured and dried meats**, **cheeses,** and the quintessential **alcoholic beverages** such as **ales, wines,** and **whiskey**. This careful selection was driven by their need to maintain a reliable and safe diet in an era where foodborne illnesses like typhoid fever, cholera, and dysentery were rampant due to poor sanitation practices.

For example, at **44 New Levee,** proprietor **G. Dorsey** offered an impressive assortment of goods essential for their daily needs. Dorsey's establishment sold everything from **fresh flour** and **lard** to an extensive selection of **whiskeys, English ales, Madeira wines** from Spain and Portugal, and robust **Claret wines** from France. The diversity and quality of products available at Dorsey's shop and others provided Will and Charles with access to preserved foods and beverages that could be safely stored and consumed, minimizing the risk of illness from spoiled or contaminated food.

Additionally, Will and Charles relied heavily on *The True American,* a prominent local newspaper of the time, to navigate the city's commercial landscape. The newspaper served as an invaluable resource, featuring detailed listings of various shops and their available products. Prominently displayed near the front page was a schedule of ships making port calls, often accompanied by inventories of the **goods** and **products** these vessels would bring. This information enabled Will and Charles to anticipate the arrival of fresh and specialty items, ensuring they could procure the best possible provisions for their needs.

By meticulously selecting their food sources and leveraging local resources like *The True American*, Will and Charles successfully navigated the complex and often hazardous culinary environment of 1830s New Orleans. Their preference for high-quality, preserved foods and strategic avoidance of less reputable eateries allowed them to maintain their health and well-being amidst the vibrant yet challenging backdrop of the antebellum South. This approach not only safeguarded them from the prevalent health risks of the time but also provided them with the flexibility to sustain themselves independently in a period marked by limited medical knowledge and widespread disease.

• • • •

Alcohol: Clarets, Madeira Wines, Ales and Whiskeys:

Madeira Wines:

Madeira wine is a fortified wine that originates from the Madeira Islands, an autonomous region of Portugal located in the North Atlantic Ocean. Renowned for its remarkable longevity and unique flavor profile, Madeira has a storied history and distinct production methods that set it apart from other wines.

Claret Wines:

Claret wines are a traditional type of red wine that originated from the Bordeaux region of France. The term "Claret" is primarily used in

British English to describe these wines, which are renowned for their elegance, complexity, and versatility. Unlike specific grape varieties, Claret refers to a style of wine, typically a blend of several Bordeaux grape varieties such as **Cabernet Sauvignon**, **Merlot**, **Cabernet Franc**, **Petit Verdot**, and **Malbec**. These blends are crafted to achieve a harmonious balance of flavors, tannins, and acidity, making Claret wines both robust and refined.

Beer-Ales:

Because New Orleans was the largest port in the Antebellum South, coupled with the influx of products from all over the world available in its shops and along the portside, beer—especially high-quality ales—was both easy to procure and exceptionally tasty, assuming you enjoyed beer. Ales from both the United Kingdom and the Northeast United States were particularly esteemed for their superior quality. Notably, the **Vassar Brewery** in Poughkeepsie, New York, was renowned for producing some of the finest beers of the day. Vassar Ale offered a limited but sophisticated range, including **Single Ale** and **Double Ale**. The **Double Ale** was further categorized into subtypes such as **Amber Double Ale** and **Pale Double Ale**, each tailored for specific markets—whether for local consumption, shipping to distant ports, or storage before use. This specialization allowed Vassar Brewery to dominate the market with robust Double Ales boasting high gravity and an average alcohol by volume (ABV) of around 8%, setting them apart from their British counterparts, where only about 20% of ale output was similarly strong.

For temporal travelers in the 1830s, accessing high-quality ales in New Orleans would not only be feasible but also a delightful experience. The city's diverse population and status as the largest port in the Antebellum South ensured a steady influx of premium ales from both the Northeast United States and Europe.

Whiskeys:

In the bustling trade economy of 1830s New Orleans, whiskey and New England rum played fascinating roles, weaving together local and international markets. Whiskey, primarily sourced from the burgeoning distilleries of Kentucky and Tennessee, was a staple in the port city's taverns and trading posts. It symbolized the growing influence of the American frontier, reflecting the westward expansion of agriculture and distilling practices. Meanwhile, New England rum arrived from northern ports, a vestige of the Atlantic triangular trade that linked the Northeast to sugar plantations in the Caribbean. Both spirits embodied a blend of tradition and innovation, fueling not only New Orleans' social scene but also its economy. They underscored the city's position as a vibrant crossroads where cultures and commodities collided, enriching its already dynamic character.

Remember!

Alcohol in the 1830s, from many of the small taverns, coffee houses, and cabarets in New Orleans, can be of questionable quality. On Gallatin Street, for example, drinks might even be laced with additives designed to knock out patrons for the purpose of robbing them. Extreme discretion is advised.

Alcohol Consumption in the 1830s US:

In the early years of the United States, alcohol consumption is strikingly high compared to modern standards. By 1790, the average drinking-age individual consumes 5.8 gallons of absolute alcohol annually—a figure that surges to an astonishing 7.1 gallons by 1830. For comparison, modern estimates suggest that Americans now consume an average of 2.3 gallons per person annually. This stark difference underscores a culture in the 1830s where heavy drinking is deeply ingrained in daily life, from social gatherings and business dealings to casual meals.

In New Orleans, this "thirsty" culture is especially pronounced. Drinking often starts at breakfast, continues through business meetings, and punctuates nearly every social or professional interaction. The city's abundance of taverns, salons, and coffee houses caters to this demand, operating extensively during the day and staying open late into the night. Alcohol is readily available, with home-brewed ales, whiskey, and other strong spirits flowing freely, making the city's drinking culture practically a 24-hour affair.

For temporal visitors, the normalization of such frequent and high-volume alcohol consumption, combined with the lack of awareness of health risks, may come as a shock. Alcohol is viewed not as a potential hazard but as an essential staple of life. The bustling taverns of New Orleans, filled with patrons enjoying strong beverages at all hours, stand in stark contrast to today's more regulated and health-conscious drinking practices.

Witnessing this unrestrained drinking culture firsthand offers a unique perspective on the social fabric of the 1830s. It reveals how deeply alcohol is woven into the routines and interactions of the era, reflecting societal norms that have undergone profound transformation. This immersion into the past highlights not only the centrality of alcohol in daily life at the time but also the significant evolution in attitudes, health awareness, and regulations surrounding alcohol consumption over the centuries.

Entertainment- Balls and Theaters

For temporal visitors seeking to truly embrace and immerse themselves in 1830s New Orleans' entertainment, a masquerade ball is an experience not to be missed. These grand events are held in many of the high-end hotels of the time, providing an evening of music, dancing, and opulent socialization. A particularly notable venue not located in a hotel is the **Washington Ballroom** on St. Philip Street, nestled between Bourbon and Royal Streets. The proprietor promises guests the finest quality liquors and food, making it a favorite destination for those in search of an unforgettable night.

However, be advised that attending a ball in the early 19th century is not a casual affair. These events are governed by strict traditions, elaborate customs, and meticulous etiquette, which will undoubtedly feel extravagant and unfamiliar to visitors from future centuries. From the intricate rules of dance and dress to the proper forms of address and behavior, every aspect of the evening is steeped in decorum.

In Book Three of *Retrorsum:* **Las Vegas Revisited**, Will and Charles attend a New Year's Eve ball in 1830s New Orleans. Their experience serves as a crash course in the rigorous etiquette of the era but is fraught with embarrassing missteps. Their night of attempted cultural immersion ultimately ends in failure, a sobering reminder of the challenges time travelers face when navigating the social complexities of a bygone age.

For temporal visitors seeking the pinnacle of 1830s New Orleans entertainment, the **St. Charles Theatre** is an absolute must-see. Opened on November 30, 1835, by the visionary James Caldwell, this grand venue stands as the crowning jewel of the city's cultural scene. Designed by Antonio Mondelli, the theatre is an architectural marvel, boasting a facade adorned with statues of Apollo and the muses, and an opulent interior featuring 4,000 seats, silk-draped boxes, and gilded columns flanking a massive 90-by-95-foot stage—likely the largest in the country. Its centerpiece, a stunning chandelier with 23,000 crystal prisms illuminated by 176 gas jets, casts a dazzling glow over every performance.

Known as "The Temple of the Drama," the St. Charles Theatre hosts productions that range from classic tragedies and comedies to melodramas, operas, and even variety acts like acrobatics and horse shows. Caldwell's star-studded programming attracts the finest actors and performers, offering an experience unparalleled in the Southeast. Whether you enjoy the elegant overtures of a 29-piece orchestra, the wit of plays like The School for Scandal, or the sheer spectacle of world-class theatrical talent, the St. Charles Theatre promises an unforgettable evening.

A word of caution for future visitors: this grand cultural hub met an untimely end on March 13, 1842, when a fire destroyed the theatre. Be sure to enjoy its splendor while you can—its legacy, much like the era it embodies, is fleeting yet magnificent.

The Camp Street Theatre, also known as the American Theatre or Old American Theatre, was a prominent venue in New Orleans from 1824 to 1835, renowned as the finest English-speaking theater in the South and celebrated for being the city's first building equipped with gas lighting. Records suggest that it was replaced by James H. Caldwell's grand St. Charles Theatre and the New American Theatre, both of which tragically burned down in 1842.

However, intriguing discrepancies exist in historical accounts. According to the *True American* newspaper in 1839, the Camp Street Theatre was still operational alongside the St. Charles Theatre, suggesting its continued role in New Orleans' vibrant cultural scene. This puzzling inconsistency is noted by Will Patterson in *Retrorsum*: **Las Vegas Revisited**. In Book Three, Will highlights this contradiction as part of his exploration of the era's theatrical legacy, offering readers a fascinating glimpse into the complexities of temporal history and the records left behind.

Visitors traveling to the 1830s are encouraged to explore both theaters, as they appear to coexist in this lively period, providing unparalleled access to the best of New Orleans' entertainment.

For those seeking the thrill of horse racing, both the **Metairie** and **Eclipse** racetracks in 1830s New Orleans are must-visit destinations. These venues offer an exhilarating opportunity to witness some of the finest thoroughbred racing action of the era, where speed, skill, and competition come together in an unforgettable spectacle.

A distinct advantage awaits temporal visitors equipped with **PDFs of the *True American*** newspaper, which frequently publishes racing results for both tracks. Armed with these historical insights, time travelers can analyze previous performances and trends, giving them a significant edge when placing bets. This invaluable resource could transform wagering from a casual pastime into a potentially profitable venture, all while enjoying the vibrant energy of the racetrack.

Be advised, however, that attending a horse race in this era is as much about the social scene as it is about the competition. Dressing appropriately is essential, as these events are vibrant displays of fashion and status. High society attendees often don their finest attire, using the occasion to showcase their wealth and standing. Whether you choose to mingle with the well-heeled crowd or simply observe the pomp and circumstance from the sidelines, immersing yourself in the culture of 1830s racetrack society promises to be a fascinating experience.

Gallatin Street- New Orleans

The following is a blend of description and partly an excerpt from *Retrorsum, Book Three*, Las Vegas Revisited where Will Patterson makes a daring visit to Gallatin Street:

If one had to pick out three famous or infamous drinking districts in US history, they would likely include the Five Points in New York City, the Barbary Coast in San Francisco, and for New Orleans, unquestionably, Gallatin Street. As a temporal visitor to 1830s New Orleans, you will find Gallatin Street to be a bustling and intimidating hub of relentless alcohol consumption and vibrant yet perilous nightlife. Arriving even as early as 3:30 PM, you'll navigate its proximity to the river and docks, with a large market not far off, setting the stage for the chaotic atmosphere that defines this infamous street.

*Upon entering Gallatin Street, you will immediately notice the overwhelming array of **cabarets**, **drinking establishments**, and **coffee houses**, each exuding its own unique character. Your options will include joints like the **GreenTree** (not to be confused with the Green Door), **The Amsterdam**, **The Baltimore**, **Archie Murphy's**, and the **Bluelight Coffee House**. The sheer number of venues, many without names, adds to the chaotic and unregulated vibe of the area, making it difficult to choose where to step in first.*

*One establishment you might enter could be the most disgusting place you've ever been to—period. This no-name joint reeks of an outhouse, with a trough beneath the bar where men urinate while standing at the bar. The combination of convenience and abominable conditions will undoubtedly make you want to leave immediately. Instead, you might opt for a beer at **Archie Murphy's**, where the only redeeming quality is the presence of beer. Here, you'll encounter bums and derelicts of every caliber, along with unfamiliar and overpowering smells. Ordering a stout beer that is both good and strong will remind you briefly of more respectable* *establishments, but make no mistake, this is Gallatin Street, where caution is highly advised the whole time you're here!*

*The women on Gallatin Street are undoubtedly the most hardened ladies you'll ever come across. While standing at the bar, a woman named Anne(for example), originally from England or Scotland, will approach you bluntly, asking for a "bub" (beer). Her strange accent—a mix of Irish and Scottish influences blended with the English of the era—will be intriguing yet challenging to understand. As you converse, Anne's initial hardness will soften, indicating a growing trust. She will share that she has been working at **Archie Murphy's** for just two months and will observe your cautious behavior, hinting at the questionable characters running around the area. Gallatin Street is the real deal, akin to the Five Points in NYC—this neighborhood will swallow you up and spit you back out if you're not careful.*

*About 20 minutes later, Anne's friends will join you, displaying a keen interest in your presence after hearing you speak. One of them, named **Zephirine**, a brunette and the oldest among them, will approach you with suspicion, interrogating you about your origins. Sharing your fabricated story of being a professor at Brown University in Providence, you'll navigate their intense curiosity. These women, capable of holding their liquor impressively, will lead you to buy a few rounds of rum or potent firewater, though you might stick mostly with your beer. The presence of women with really bad teeth will highlight the daunting prospect of visiting a dentist in that era, while the clientele's intent on getting drunk as quickly as possible will emphasize the high alcohol intake prevalent on Gallatin Street.*

About 10 minutes later, a man will stroll up with a massive jug of what seems to be rum or whiskey, passing it around among himself and the ladies. The relentless drinking will be something you don't see often, and despite your initial refusals, you might eventually take a swig of the strong and unpleasant-tasting liquor. As the evening progresses, the place will grow rowdy with people passing out on the floor and dancing breaking out, even though it's only around 6 PM. This chaotic environment will signal your cue to leave as soon as possible.

Gallatin Street is, without a doubt, one of the most infamous drinking districts in US history, rivaling places like the Five Points and the Barbary Coast. Its relentless alcohol consumption, diverse and often unsanitary establishments, and the hardened characters that frequent the street create an environment that is both fascinating and perilous for any temporal visitor. Navigating Gallatin Street requires caution and awareness, as the high volume of alcohol consumed by the people of this era will likely leave you both shocked and astonished by the sheer intensity and frequency of drinking.

For any daring temporal visitor to **Gallatin Street**, vigilance and caution cannot be overstated. If you decide to make a visit, it is probably best to go during the daytime. While the sights and experiences will be no less exciting than a nighttime visit, the daylight will at least offer you some semblance of security and make it easier to navigate your way back to the hotel where you are staying. Even in the daytime, however, Gallatin Street is not for the faint-hearted—it is a place where grime and chaos rule, and surprises lurk around every corner.

The entertainment on Gallatin Street goes beyond the relentless alcohol consumption. Visitors will witness spectacles that range from intriguing to utterly appalling, including **cockfighting** and, shockingly, **dogfighting**. These violent forms of "entertainment" are common attractions in this lawless district, drawing raucous crowds eager to gamble and revel in the savage contests. The sounds of men shouting, bets being placed, and the visceral energy of the crowd create a grim atmosphere that might leave modern visitors both disturbed and fascinated. Such activities, while normalized in the antebellum South, underscore the raw and often brutal nature of life in this era. For the temporal visitor, they serve as a stark reminder of the profound cultural differences between the 1830s and the modern world. A visit to

Gallatin Street is not just a venture into New Orleans' notorious past but a visceral immersion into the unfiltered realities of an era where entertainment often came at a cost to morality and civility.

For the temporal visitor daring to venture to Gallatin Street, understanding the establishments you'll encounter is crucial for both safety and context. The street features two predominant types of venues: **barrel houses** and **dance houses**, each catering to the vices and indulgences of its patrons in distinct, yet equally notorious, ways.

Barrel houses are as grim as their name implies. These long, narrow rooms are lined with barrels of liquor, each fitted with a spigot. For just five cents, patrons can fill their glasses from any barrel they choose. However, these are no artisanal spirits—these liquors are cheap, dangerous concoctions, often spiked with dubious and harmful additives. Without modern oversight like the FDA, substances such as **sulphuric acid** or **chewing tobacco** were sometimes used to enhance the color or flavor of whiskey. Unsurprisingly, these additives posed severe health risks, and the liquor itself could easily incapacitate even seasoned drinkers. Adding to the dangers, barrel house owners frequently laced drinks with **knockout drops**, enabling thieves to rob patrons once they passed out. If you stop drinking, you're unceremoniously ejected—there's no room for loitering in such a cutthroat establishment. For a temporal visitor, the experience might feel more like stepping into a trap than enjoying a drink, and vigilance is essential.

On the other hand, **dance houses** offer a livelier, though no less perilous, atmosphere. These establishments, with colorful names like the **House of Rest for Weary Boatmen**, **Mother Bunk's Den**, and the **Sure Enuf Hotel**, are a mix of bar, brothel, and dance floor. Typically housed in two- or three-story buildings, they feature bars and dance floors on the first level, while the upper floors contain small rooms rented by sex workers. These women, often hardened by the grueling life of Gallatin Street, rely solely on their earnings from **sex work** and

robbery, as they are not paid by the establishment owners. Disease, violence, and exploitation are rampant, with the average lifespan of an antebellum sex worker on Gallatin Street estimated to be just **four years**, according to historian Judith Kelleher Schafer.

For the temporal visitor, stepping into a dance house will likely be an overwhelming sensory experience. The lively music, the scent of alcohol, and the frenetic energy of the dance floor collide with the grim reality of exploitation happening behind closed doors upstairs. The women you meet here might seem bold and vivacious, but their lives are fraught with danger and hardship. Encounters with these women could range from moments of intrigue to potential peril, as the boundaries between revelry and survival blur in these establishments.

Gallatin Street is a stark reminder of the vices and challenges that defined the darker sides of antebellum society. The sheer chaos of its barrel houses and dance houses foreshadows the attempts at regulation that would later lead to the creation of **Storyville**, New Orleans' infamous red-light district, in 1897. Unlike Gallatin Street, Storyville was a more structured environment, modeled after European port-town red-light districts, where sex work was regulated and less violent. Storyville's existence from 1897 to 1917 reflects an effort to tame the wild excesses of places like Gallatin Street, offering a glimpse into how New Orleans evolved to reconcile its vices with attempts at reform. For temporal visitors, the contrast between these two eras underscores the raw, untamed nature of Gallatin Street and the human cost of its chaotic indulgences.

Remember and Understand:

Due to the limited historical documentation of Gallatin Street, any temporal visitor to this fascinating but potentially dangerous part of 1830s New Orleans must consider that many of the businesses, taverns, and other establishments mentioned here may or may not exist at the time of your visit.

Crime, Safety and Security

As with any place in any era, New Orleans of the 1830s certainly had its share of crime. As a temporal visitor to this alluring yet potentially perilous environment, it is imperative to prepare yourself accordingly. In this antebellum period, the city was alive with contrasts: though it boasted considerable wealth and served as the largest metropolis in the American South, it was also rife with poverty, disease, and desperation. The allure of its bustling port and thriving commerce attracted an eclectic mix of travelers, sailors, merchants, and fortune-seekers, but it also drew pickpockets, con artists, and other opportunistic criminals.

When navigating the bustling streets of 1830s New Orleans, it is crucial to protect your belongings—especially any modern gadgets, such as smartphones (which are not recommended in the city's side streets due to the risk of theft). Whenever possible, keep such items secured in locked trunks or safes at your place of residence, and exercise the utmost caution if you must carry them outdoors.

Taking photographs with a smartphone, in particular, can draw unwanted attention in an era utterly unfamiliar with such technology; locals and authorities alike may view it as a strange, even supernatural device. If you decide to snap any images, remain discreet: keep your phone concealed until the moment you need it, stay aware of your surroundings, and avoid using it in crowded areas such as marketplaces, wharves, and busy thoroughfares.

Should a thief successfully steal your phone, their attempts to identify or utilize the item could quickly reveal its extraordinary nature. This discovery might lead them—or anyone else who hears of it—to question who owns such a baffling contraption, thrusting you into the harsh spotlight of suspicion. To avoid such complications, vigilance and subtlety are essential, ensuring you can explore the city's lively streets without inadvertently becoming a magnet for trouble.

Before settling into any hotel or guest house, try to get a sense of its security measures. Upscale hotels typically provide some level of protection, given the high-profile clientele they serve, but it is always wise to remain cautious and keep your valuables secured.

Beyond the ever-present threat of theft, the dangers in 1830s New Orleans extend far beyond pickpockets. The city's vibrant nightlife—driven by gambling parlors, taverns, and brothels—can be rife with unsavory characters eager to deceive or rob unwary visitors. Keep a watchful eye on your surroundings, and whenever possible, avoid roaming unfamiliar districts alone, especially after nightfall.

The possibility of sustaining cuts, scrapes, and other minor injuries is a very real hazard in such a raucous and unsanitary environment, making it essential to come prepared with your own medicaments. In fact, local doctors should be avoided at all costs: their limited medical knowledge and frequently dangerous methods often pose a greater risk than the ailments themselves. By taking responsibility for your own healthcare—treating minor wounds with proper supplies kept at your place of residence, and exercising sensible caution—you can minimize your vulnerability in this lively yet perilous era.

Furthermore, any interaction with law enforcement carries its own set of perils. In the early 19th century, police forces—where they existed—were notorious for their lack of structure, oversight, and the modern procedures we take for granted today. Accusations could be made on the weakest of grounds, leaving one unjustly incarcerated or subjected to corrupt practices with little recourse. The conditions within jails and holding cells were often dismal: overcrowded, unsanitary, and rife with disease, creating an environment where a short stay behind bars could quickly become life-threatening. Legal proceedings were haphazard at best, and it was not uncommon for suspects to languish indefinitely, waiting on a trial that might never come. By minimizing contact with law enforcement and avoiding even the smallest suggestion of wrongdoing, you stand a far better chance of preserving both your freedom and your well-being during your stay in this tumultuous era.

With vigilance, solid preparations, and a keen awareness of your surroundings, you can still savor the tantalizing wonders of 1830s New Orleans—its rich cultural tapestry, vibrant music, and unparalleled culture—while minimizing the dangers inherent in this enthralling yet unpredictable time.

The St. Charles Hotel in 1838: A Luxurious Haven for Temporal Travelers:

In 1838, the brand-new **St. Charles Hotel** stands as a marvel of modern engineering and architectural grandeur in downtown New Orleans. Designed by J. Gallier and completed at a staggering cost of $600,000, this colossal edifice presents a majestic portico of **Corinthian columns** soaring from a granite base, immediately capturing the awe of all who approach. Within its walls, travelers will discover more than 300 elegantly furnished rooms spread across multiple floors, each accessed by a network of staircases—including a grand spiral stairway that culminates beneath a gleaming dome. The dome itself, perched atop fluted columns, offers breathtaking views of the winding Mississippi River and the sprawling cityscape, reminiscent of the iconic experience of beholding St. Paul's Cathedral in London. By night, the structure's distinctive silhouette and moonlit marble façade create a sight of unrivaled splendor, leaving visitors—whether local or from distant times—in absolute wonder.

Services and Amenities for the Discerning Time Traveler:

The St. Charles Hotel on St. Charles Street stands as the most reliable and luxurious option for any time traveler venturing to 1830s New Orleans. Within its grand structure, an octagonal **bar room** measuring seventy feet in diameter teems with social activity among the city's elite, while expansive **dining rooms**—capable of seating hundreds—are adorned with **Corinthian columns** and tasteful decor. For modern visitors concerned about 19th-century hygiene, the hotel offers **fourteen private bathing rooms** with hot or cold baths, ensuring a rare degree of comfort. A thoughtfully placed **kitchen** caters to a wide variety of tastes between the separate ladies' and gentlemen's dining areas, and the elegant **parlors** provide tranquil settings for conversation or respite. Together, these amenities are a testament to the St. Charles Hotel's reputation as a self-contained haven of refinement in an otherwise rugged era.

Seeking out accommodations at the St. Charles or at the **Verandah Hotel**—set to open across the street in mid 1839—will undoubtedly be the best bet for temporal visitors. Both establishments function almost like **cities within the city**, catering primarily to upper-class residents and travelers. You will find everything from **post offices**, **restaurants**, **cafés**, **taverns**, to a multitude of **shops** and **import parlors** tucked within their walls. For those looking to avoid the grime, filth, and poverty that plague much of New Orleans at this time, these hotels offer a welcome sanctuary of relative comfort and convenience for the late 1830s.

The Verandah Hotel (1839):

Completed in 1839 at a cost of $300,000, the Verandah Hotel offers a notable alternative to the grandeur of the nearby St. Charles. Designed by the architectural team of Dakin and Dakin, it showcases an early example of the long, full-width gallery that would become a familiar sight on New Orleans' streetscapes after the 1850s. This inviting upper-story gallery, supported by iron columns and lined with iron railings, is a hallmark of the Verandah's exterior. Although it lacks the dramatic dome and Corinthian flourishes of its rival across the way, its Greek Revival style imparts a sense of "chasteness and simplicity," as praised by a local writer in the 1842 *City Directory*.

Inside, however, the Verandah spares no expense in lavishness. Guests entering its **85-foot-long dining room** will find three **elliptical domes**, each designed to accommodate **gas-lit chandeliers** that lend an opulent glow to evening meals. Retail stores and offices occupy the ground floor, while four upper stories of hotel rooms stretch across several bays facing both St. Charles Avenue and Common Street. For temporal travelers seeking an alternative to the bustling St. Charles, the Verandah Hotel provides a refined yet accessible stay—complete with a balance of modest exterior elegance and indulgent interior comforts befitting this vibrant era in New Orleans' history.

In book three of Retrorsum, Las Vegas Revisited, Will Patterson takes up residence at the Verandah Hotel for the remainder of his time spent in 1839.

• • • •

The St. Louis Hotel: A French Quarter Landmark and Slave Trade Hub:

For temporal visitors to **1830s New Orleans**, the **St. Louis Hotel**—sometimes called the *City Exchange Hotel*—stands out as a significant, though deeply problematic, establishment. Located at the intersection of **St. Louis** and **Chartres** Streets in the French Quarter, it rivals the more Anglo-American St. Charles Hotel across town. With its ornate **rotunda**, grand **ballroom**, and a large **vestibule** (forty by 127 feet), the St. Louis Hotel initially appears to offer amenities comparable to other premier accommodations of the era, such as a dining hall, public parlors, and event spaces that host elegant balls. However, its true notoriety stems from being a central venue for **slave auctions**, held regularly under the soaring rotunda.

Services and Amenities in the French Quarter:

- **Ballroom and Event Spaces**: The St. Louis Hotel attracted visiting dignitaries and hosted lavish gatherings, such as the famed bal travesti where Henry Clay spoke.

- **On-Site Retail and Offices**: Like the St. Charles, it included a variety of shops and offices on the ground floor, providing guests with convenient access to commercial services.

- **Dining Facilities**: While period accounts describe an impressive dining room, any sense of luxury is overshadowed by the grievous reality of enslaved people being sold within the same complex.

- **Proximity to the French Quarter**: Occupying a large footprint along St. Louis, Chartres, and Royale Streets, the hotel was intended to be a hub of creole social life, catering to both local elites and European visitors.

Why It May Not Be Suitable for Temporal Visitors:

While the St. Louis Hotel presents a degree of upper-class comfort, it also serves as the epicenter of one of the era's greatest moral failings: the **slave trade**. Enslaved men, women, and children were brought to the building's **auction block** in full view of guests, treated as commodities to be bought and sold. This stark contradiction—sumptuous lodging and brutal human trafficking—makes staying at the St. Louis Hotel deeply uncomfortable from a modern perspective. The very design of the **rotunda** facilitated these auctions, placing enslaved individuals on display like merchandise before eager bidders.

Given these circumstances, contemporary travelers from the future may find it difficult to reconcile the hotel's opulent offerings with the horrific practices that took place within its walls. While the St. Louis Hotel stands as a piece of local history in the French Quarter, its legacy as a **slave auction hub** renders it a troubling choice for accommodations. Those concerned with the ethical ramifications of their visit may prefer other establishments—such as the St. Charles or Verandah Hotels—that, though still representative of antebellum society, do not so directly host the buying and selling of human beings under a single, grand dome.

Important Note:

*While the slave trade is especially conspicuous at the St. Louis Exchange Hotel, historical records indicate that slave auctions also take place at the St. Charles Hotel. It is crucial to remember that **slave pens and auctions are ubiquitous** throughout New Orleans during this period and **are** woven deeply into the city's daily life and economy. For temporal travelers, witnessing these practices—no matter where they occur—can be profoundly unsettling, highlighting the stark moral and cultural differences that define the antebellum era.*

Bishop's Hotel (Later Known as the City Hotel):

Originally constructed in 1832 at the intersection of Camp and Common Streets, Bishop's Hotel (soon to be renamed Richardson's Hotel, and eventually the City Hotel) is a prominent lodging choice for 1830s visitors to New Orleans, albeit overshadowed by the larger and more renowned St. Louis and St. Charles Hotels. Despite its slightly lower profile, Bishop's Hotel stands at four stories tall and occupies a bustling corner that draws a steady stream of travelers, including Texans, steamboat operators, and railroad men who favor the hotel for its convenience and hospitality.

Architecture and Ownership:

- **Designed by Charles Zimpel**: With four floors, the building showcases the functional style of the era while still providing a measure of elegance suitable for guests of moderate to higher means.

● **Name Evolution**: After opening as Bishop's Hotel, it changes ownership and names—becoming **Richardson's Hotel**—before finally being renamed the **City Hotel** around **1839–1840**.

● **Managed by Ruggles S. Morse**: A transplanted businessman from Portland, Maine, Morse not only oversees daily operations but also demonstrates civic responsibility by aiding in relief efforts during medical crises, such as providing supplies for victims of the 1862 Ponchatoula train wreck.

Services and Ambiance:

● **Lodging for Various Clientele**: Although not as opulent as the St. Charles or St. Louis, Bishop's Hotel appeals to middle- and upper-tier travelers seeking comfortable accommodations without the bustle of the city's grandest establishments. Texans and steamboat crews, in particular, favor the hotel for its relaxed atmosphere.

● **Dining and Social Life**: Guests can expect traditional Southern fare and a sociable environment, reflecting the broader custom of New Orleans hotels serving as hubs for civic gatherings and leisurely meals.

Connection to the Slave Trade:

● **Slave Auctions on the Premises**: Like many major antebellum hotels, Bishop's Hotel (later the City Hotel) also hosts **slave auctions**, a stark reminder of the era's moral and social realities. These auctions occasionally take place within the hotel's public spaces, paralleling practices at the St. Louis and St. Charles Hotels.

● **Uncomfortable Reality for Modern Visitors**: For temporal travelers, this aspect of Bishop's Hotel underscores the pervasive nature of slavery in 1830s New Orleans, presenting a sobering insight into the city's economic and social structure.

Why Choose Bishop's Hotel?:

1. **Central Location**: Situated near major thoroughfares, the hotel provides convenient access to commerce, river traffic, and other points of interest.
2. **Moderate Luxury**: Although less grand than the St. Charles or St. Louis, Bishop's Hotel offers a comfortable stay, making it suitable for travelers seeking a blend of amenities without the highest expense.
3. **Cultural Insight**: Bishop's Hotel grants a unique vantage point into the city's antebellum character, particularly its bustling business dealings and constant influx of travelers—a microcosm of New Orleans' broader social landscape.

*In Book Three of **Retrorsum: Las Vegas Revisited**, both Will and Charles attend a lottery drawing at this hotel on December 13, 1838. With access to future knowledge, they use their advantage to acquire currency appropriate to the era.*

Mrs. Anderson's Boarding House:

Located at the corner of **Poydras and St. Charles Streets**, close to the landmark **St. Charles Theater**, *Mrs. Anderson's Boarding House* presents an alternative for temporal travelers who wish to experience the charm—and more typical living standards—of **1830s New Orleans** without the opulence of the city's grand hotels. Here, guests can immerse themselves in the era's everyday rhythms and social customs, gaining insight into the lives of ordinary residents rather than the elite clientele frequenting luxury establishments.

However, **official records** for Mrs. Anderson's Boarding House are scarce or entirely **nonexistent**. As a result, travelers should proceed with **extreme caution** if considering this accommodation. Unlike the well-documented St. Charles or St. Louis Hotels, Mrs. Anderson's lacks verified historical data on amenities, pricing, or safety. Consequently, while it may offer an authentic taste of antebellum New Orleans life, prospective guests should be prepared for potential uncertainties and discomforts inherent to less formal lodging arrangements of the time.

Other Alternatives:

For temporal travelers exploring **1830s New Orleans**, additional accommodation options extend beyond the renowned luxury hotels of the day. Numerous **boarding houses, guesthouses, and smaller inns** are scattered throughout the city, offering a range of experiences for those seeking a place to stay. To locate these establishments, visitors are encouraged to consult local publications of the era, such as the **New Orleans Bee** or the **True American**, which regularly feature advertisements and listings for various lodging options.

However, as emphasized earlier, travelers arriving from several centuries in the future must exercise **careful consideration** when selecting accommodations. These establishments, while potentially charming and historically immersive, may not meet modern expectations for cleanliness, safety, or comfort. Many are privately operated, with minimal oversight, making it essential to use discretion when choosing where to stay. Furthermore, **understanding the norms and practices of the era**, such as shared facilities and modest furnishings, will help manage expectations and ensure a smoother experience. For travelers who value security and reliability, sticking to **better-documented options** like the St. Charles, Verandah or St. Louis Hotels might still be the wiser choice.

Restaurants and Eateries

For the most part, confining your meals to the eateries within the more upscale hotels is your safest and most practical option. Not only do these establishments offer a wider variety of dishes, but they also provide a **relatively** higher standard of food safety compared to local cafes and street vendors. However, it is crucial to remember that even these upscale establishments operate without the benefit of modern sanitary practices. Concepts like sterilization, proper refrigeration, and hygiene standards are virtually non-existent in the 1830s, making the potential for foodborne illness a constant risk.

In **book three of *Retrorsum, Las Vegas Revisited*,** both Will and Charles wisely confine their meals to pre-prepared dried foods, cured meats, cheeses, and other preserved items for their daily sustenance. This strategy not only minimizes the risk of illness but also ensures a consistent intake of familiar and safe food. Their cautious approach highlights the importance of understanding and adapting to the limitations of food hygiene in the antebellum period.

It cannot be overstated how vital it is for temporal travelers to exercise **extreme caution** regarding food choices. Many local cafes, coffee houses, and small eateries—though potentially tempting with their local flair—often lack even the rudimentary cleanliness of the upscale hotels of the era. Such establishments may present not only a risk of gastrointestinal distress but also exposure to more severe illnesses such as typhoid, cholera, or dysentery. For those who value their health and ability to continue their journey, sticking to safer, well-prepared options remains a priority.

Important Note:

*For all temporal travelers, **under no circumstances** should you drink the local water in 1830s New Orleans without taking proper precautions.*

The water supply during this era is notoriously unsafe, often contaminated with harmful bacteria, parasites, and pollutants. Diseases like cholera and dysentery are common in the city, making untreated water a potential health hazard. If you intend to consume local water, it is imperative to first boil it thoroughly or ensure that water purification tablets were among the essential items in your travel preparations.

Hot beverages like coffee and tea served in the cafes of upscale hotels are generally considered safer options, as the boiling process involved in their preparation can eliminate many contaminants. However, even in these establishments, it is wise to remain cautious. Ensure that the beverages are freshly prepared and served hot, as lukewarm drinks might not have undergone sufficient heating to kill harmful microorganisms.

As a temporal visitor, safeguarding your health is paramount. Consider relying on bottled beverages—like ales, wines—or consuming drinks you have brought with you from the present. (assuming you did)

If you are someone who abstains from alcoholic beverages, navigating the options for safe, non-alcoholic drinks in 1830s New Orleans can present a unique challenge. In an era where water is virtually unsafe to consume and sanitation practices are primative, finding trustworthy alternatives may require creativity and effort.

One potential option is to make your own fresh fruit juices. This approach, however, comes with its own set of precautions. Begin by ensuring you thoroughly wash all fruit with boiled or purified water before peeling it. The exterior of the fruit may carry contaminants from the local environment, so this step is crucial. Once washed, peel the fruit carefully, as the outer layers are more likely to harbor bacteria or other impurities. If you have access to a safe, clean space for preparation, you can then juice the fruit to create a refreshing and relatively safe beverage.

This process assumes you have the necessary tools and access to fresh, high-quality fruit—a luxury that may not always be readily available in 1830s New Orleans, depending on your accommodations and circumstances. As an alternative, consider carrying portable water purification tools or bringing powdered drink mixes that can be prepared with boiled water. Both options offer greater convenience and ensure a measure of safety.

Navigating the drink options of the time requires vigilance, resourcefulness, and planning. With these precautions in place, you can still enjoy hydrating beverages while maintaining your health and well-being during your temporal journey.

Local Markets in 1830s New Orleans

Exploring the Markets of 1830s New Orleans: A Temporal Visitor's Delight:

For temporal travelers venturing into 1830s New Orleans, the city's vibrant network of public markets offers a captivating glimpse into daily life and culture. Strolling through these bustling hubs of commerce and community interaction allows you to experience the authentic sights, sounds, and smells of the era while admiring the unique architectural and historical landmarks that define New Orleans.

French Market (Meat and Vegetable Market):

As the oldest and most enduring market in New Orleans, the French Market is already a cornerstone of the city in the 1830s. Located along the Mississippi River in the French Quarter, this market teems with vendors offering meats, vegetables, and other essentials. Its lively atmosphere, infused with French, Spanish, Creole, and Caribbean influences, creates a vibrant and colorful experience. For temporal visitors, the French Market is an essential stop to immerse in the multicultural roots of the city.

Poydras Market:

Opened in 1837 on Poydras Street, this market is a testament to the city's growth and dynamism. Situated between Baronne and South Rampart Streets, its proximity to the Carrollton Railroad ensures easy transportation of goods, making it a bustling hub for both prominent families and everyday citizens. Vendors here offer fresh produce, household goods, and more, all within an organized, lively setting that reflects the energy of a city on the rise.

St. Mary's Market:

Located in the Faubourg St. Mary suburb on Tchoupitoulas Street, St. Mary's Market serves as a major commercial hub in the American Sector. Expanded in 1830 and 1836, it exemplifies the era's emphasis on practicality and design. Created by architect Joseph Pilie, the market stands as an important stop for locals and travelers alike, offering a wide array of goods in a vibrant setting that showcases the evolving needs of a growing city.

Washington Market:

Located in the downriver Faubourg Marigny neighborhood, Washington Market opens in 1838, catering to the diverse local community. Nestled at the top of the Marigny Triangle, where Esplanade and Elysian Fields Avenues converge, this market—originally called the Port Market when it opened in 1835—serves as a charming spot for temporal visitors. Its triangular layout and river views make it a picturesque location for exploring the culture of antebellum New Orleans.

Tremé Market:

Built earlier in the 1830s, the Tremé Market on Orleans Avenue between Marais and North Robertson Streets thrives as a center of Creole culture and community. A lively gathering place filled with music, chatter, and a diverse array of goods, the market reflects the rich cultural tapestry of New Orleans. Temporal visitors will find themselves immersed in the rhythms of this historic neighborhood, which remains a vibrant cultural hub.

<u>Interesting Fact!</u>

Although Bourbon Street exists in 1830s New Orleans, it is not the raucous partying street we know today. In the early 1800s, Bourbon Street is primarily residential, lacking the lively nightlife and entertainment venues that define it in modern times. The transformation of Bourbon Street into the bustling, vibrant hub of nightlife began in the early 1900s.

The Banks Arcade:

For temporal visitors exploring late 1830s New Orleans, **Banks' Arcade** is a must-see landmark that encapsulates the city's commercial vibrancy and social dynamism during this era. Located on Magazine Street between Gravier and Natchez Streets, this impressive three-story structure, designed by architect Charles F. Zimpel, was one of the most significant commercial buildings of its time. Its defining feature, a central glass-covered arcade, not only divided the building but also gave it its distinctive name, creating an elegant and airy thoroughfare that enhanced its grandeur.

The ground floor of Banks' Arcade housed offices for attorneys and brokers, while its true allure lay in John Hewlett's renowned "grand coffee room," a bustling restaurant and social hub. Here, locals and visitors gathered to discuss the events of the day, sip coffee, and enjoy the energy of antebellum New Orleans. The second floor offered billiard rooms and served as the armory for the Washington Guards, adding a layer of intrigue for military history enthusiasts. Meanwhile, the third floor operated as a gentlemen-only hotel, providing accommodations for travelers seeking refined lodging.

Banks' Arcade was also a venue for historic gatherings, such as the October 1835 meeting of the **Friends of Texas**, which responded to General Sam Houston's call for volunteers in the Texas Revolution. This pivotal assembly led to the formation of the New Orleans Greys, a valiant group whose sacrifices at the Battle of the Alamo and Goliad Massacre remain etched in history. Temporal visitors with a penchant for historic moments will find the arcade's rich legacy both captivating and poignant.

Orleans Parish Prison:

For temporal visitors to 1830s New Orleans, the Old Parish Prison in the Tremé neighborhood offers a stark and sobering glimpse into the city's justice system of the era. Designed by architects Joseph Pilié and A. Voilquin and constructed between 1831 and 1836, the prison boasts an austere Franco-Spanish aesthetic. Its stuccoed walls and long arcades exude a foreboding presence, while interior courtyards and galleries reinforce the grim functionality of the space. Separate cell blocks are designated according to offenses, reflecting a rudimentary yet organized approach to incarceration. The building's two cupolas rise above the hipped roof, punctuating the skyline, and sycamore trees lining the compound walls offer a deceptive air of tranquility.

Built in 1834, the prison also housed a gallows, serving as a site for public executions that often drew crowds. These grim spectacles underscored the harsh realities of justice in the 19th century and the macabre interest such events garnered among locals. Over the decades, the prison's reputation darkened further, culminating in the 1891 massacre of 11 Italian-Americans, who were kidnapped and lynched by a mob in what remains one of the most infamous incidents in New Orleans' history.

By the end of the 19th century, the prison's Dickensian aura and inhumane living conditions led to its condemnation. As the city expanded upriver and modernized, the outdated facility was deemed inadequate, and it was finally razed in 1895. For temporal visitors, the Old Parish Prison offers not just a lesson in architecture and societal structure but also a sobering reminder of the brutal realities and prejudices of the era. While the sycamore-lined walls might hint at serenity, the stories held within them reveal a far grimmer tale of punishment and injustice.

New Orleans and Carrollton Railroad:

If you are a railroad enthusiast, one truly fascinating experience for temporal visitors to 1830s New Orleans is the New Orleans and Carrollton Railroad. This line offers a unique glimpse into the early stages of railroad technology and engineering, showcasing a time when horse and mule power served as the backbone of urban transit innovation. Established in 1835, the New Orleans and Carrollton Railroad connects the burgeoning small community of Carrollton to the bustling city center of New Orleans, specifically to the area now known as Lee Circle.

The railroad began as a simple, animal-driven line, but it quickly became a vital transportation artery for commuters. Carrollton, which would later be incorporated as a town in 1845 and annexed by New Orleans in 1874, was one of the first true bedroom suburbs of the city. Initially, the community attracted wealthy New Orleanians seeking a tranquil retreat in its lush gardens and attractions like the Carrollton Hotel. As the area grew and evolved, so too did the railroad, transitioning from a leisurely ride for visitors to a crucial commuter service for residents traveling to and from New Orleans.

For temporal visitors, the New Orleans and Carrollton Railroad offers more than just a historical curiosity—it provides an authentic experience of life and innovation in the 1830s. The sight of mule- or horse-drawn railcars traversing the city's streets and countryside highlights the ingenuity of the era and the beginnings of suburban development in America. Whether you're a dedicated railroad enthusiast or simply curious about early transportation, a ride or observation of this line offers a memorable and enlightening journey through the past.

Before embarking on any journey beyond 1830s New Orleans, a temporal visitor must first consider the modes of transportation available at the time. Railroads may exist, but they remain in their infancy and offer severely limited routes. Consequently, most travelers rely on packet sailing ships, steamers, and stagecoaches to reach destinations both nearby and far-flung.

To find the most up-to-date schedules and fares, consult period newspapers such as the **True American** or the **New Orleans Bee**. These publications regularly list ships departing from New Orleans' busy port, including those bound for the Northeast—such as New York and Philadelphia—as well as vessels heading to Savannah or crossing the Atlantic to Havre and Liverpool. Other ships journey southward, stopping at ports in Havana, Jamaica, and even venturing as far west as the Republic of Texas. Keep in mind that travel times during this era could be quite lengthy; a trip to the Northeast alone might take 11 to 13 days, depending on weather conditions and the vessel's efficiency.

For those who prefer land travel, stagecoaches remain a viable, albeit slower, option. Roads can be unreliable—dusty in dry weather, muddy in rain, and riddled with hazards. Meanwhile, steamers ply the rivers, offering somewhat faster passage than stagecoaches but carrying their own risks, such as mechanical failures or boiler explosions.

Regardless of your chosen method, be mindful that each journey is prone to delays, harsh conditions, and the inherent unpredictability of 19th-century travel. Adequate preparation, familiarity with timetables, and a solid dose of patience are essential when venturing out of New Orleans during this formative and often tumultuous era.

In Book Three of *Retrorsum: Las Vegas Revisited*, Will Patterson, with over half a year remaining in 1839, dares to embark on a packet ship bound for New York City. From there, he undertakes an 18-day voyage across the North Atlantic aboard the **SS Liverpool**, ultimately landing in Liverpool, England, before pressing on to Scotland.

For shorter excursions, river steamers offer relatively swift travel from New Orleans up to Baton Rouge, Natchez, Vicksburg, and Memphis. Yet travelers must remember that river navigation during this period brims with peril: hidden snags from submerged logs can cripple or sink vessels, and boiler technology remains in its infancy, leading to alarming rates of boiler explosions. These hazards underscore the importance of vigilance, practical preparedness, and a healthy respect for the often unforgiving waterways of the era.

Another option for travel includes the wide variety of vessels that navigate routes to western destinations such as the Republic of Texas or eastward to ports like Pensacola, Mobile, and Apalachicola. These routes provide intriguing opportunities to explore different regions, but they also carry significant risks and challenges, especially for temporal explorers venturing into less developed territories.

Remember!

Many of these ports of call are small and underdeveloped during this time, particularly those heading west into the Republic of Texas. This region, along with the broader western frontier, is in the very early stages of settlement. The rule of law is tenuous at best, and a rugged, frontier-like environment dominates these areas. Temporal explorers must recognize that venturing into such locations means confronting a volatile mix of lawlessness, hardship, and isolation.

Dangers and Pitfalls:

1. **Lawlessness and Hostility**: The Republic of Texas and other frontier regions are notorious for their lack of organized law enforcement. Vigilante justice and local disputes can quickly escalate into violence. Additionally, territorial tensions with Mexico and ongoing conflicts with Indigenous nations make the region especially perilous.

2. **Sparse Resources:** Settlements in these areas are few and far between, with limited access to supplies, medical care, or reliable lodging. Temporal explorers must come equipped with their own provisions and tools, as local infrastructure is unlikely to meet even basic needs.

3. **Travel Hazards:** Traveling by sea to these smaller ports carries risks inherent to 19th-century maritime transport, including storms, uncharted waters, and subpar ship maintenance. Once on land, overland routes are often crude trails susceptible to weather-related disruptions, bandit attacks, or dangerous wildlife.

4. **Unpredictability:** The frontier's unpredictability cannot be overstated. Sudden conflicts, accidents, or natural disasters could leave you stranded without recourse. Unlike established cities—where, in this time period, assistance is often inadequate or worse than the emergency itself—survival on the frontier depends even more heavily on quick thinking and self-reliance. The dangers are far more precarious, and any traveler must understand that if you choose to venture this far out, you are essentially on your own.

5. **Additionally,** one must carefully consider the level of

unpredictability in transportation and factor in the time required to return to your point of departure and, ultimately, your means of return to the present. Misjudging travel times or encountering delays could result in being stranded in an unforgiving and dangerous environment, underscoring the need for meticulous planning and a keen awareness of the risks involved.

Advice for Temporal Explorers:

● **Plan Meticulously**: Research your intended destination thoroughly and ensure you have an exit strategy should conditions become unsafe.

● **Travel Light and Smart**: Bring only what you can carry efficiently, but prioritize essential supplies such as food, water purification tools, and medical kits.

● **Build Local Alliances(where possible)**: Seek out trusted locals or fellow travelers who can offer guidance and support. Knowledge of the area is invaluable in mitigating risks.

● **Avoid Drawing Attention**: Stay inconspicuous to avoid becoming a target for theft or unwanted scrutiny.

Exploring the frontier can be a fascinating and rewarding experience, but it requires thorough preparation and a healthy respect for the dangers that lie beyond the relative safety of established ports and cities. With caution and planning, temporal explorers can navigate these perilous territories while minimizing the risks inherent to such a bold endeavor.

Conclusions

<u>Last Notes:</u>

The goal of this *Time Travelers' Handbook* is to serve as a helpful and practical guide for temporal visitors venturing to the late 1830s, focusing specifically on the captivating city of New Orleans during the years 1838-1839. This guide aims to equip travelers with the knowledge, insights, and tips necessary to navigate this dynamic period with confidence and curiosity.

As with any travel guide—whether for journeys across space or time—it is impossible to anticipate every situation, location, or interaction a traveler might encounter. However, this handbook strives to provide a thoughtful overview, offering vital context, preparation for potential challenges, and highlights of the extraordinary sights, sounds, and experiences available in this fascinating but complex era.

The late 1830s in New Orleans was a time of unparalleled vibrancy, cultural convergence, and growth, but also a period shadowed by profound societal challenges and tragedies. From the grandeur of the St. Charles Theatre and the thrill of horse racing at the Metairie and Eclipse racetracks to the charm of masquerade balls and the bustling energy of the port, New Orleans during this period offers an abundance of captivating experiences. At the same time, visitors will encounter the stark realities of a society grappling with inequality, public health crises, and the stark divisions of the Antebellum South.

It is not the intent of this guide to scare or invoke fear in temporal travelers wanting to visit 1830s New Orleans. Rather, this handbook aims to provide essential "heads up" information to help navigate this extraordinary yet challenging time in history. Awareness of the cultural norms, social structures, and potential hazards of this period will allow travelers to engage meaningfully with the era while minimizing unnecessary risks.

For temporal travelers, the opportunity to witness life in late 1830s New Orleans firsthand is both a privilege and a responsibility. It's a chance to immerse oneself in the city's lively rhythms, to appreciate the resilience and creativity of its inhabitants, and to reflect on the rich yet turbulent history that shaped this remarkable time and place.

Advisory:

It is important to keep this handbook both protected and concealed with appropriate sleeve or cover!!

<u>Information Sources:</u>

Library of Congress - Chronicling America-Newspapers
The True American- New Orleans, Louisiana 1838-1839

# About the Author

Derrick Fitzgerald, the author of the new book titled "Retrorsum," has dedicated many years to extensive travels from the early 1980s to the present day. His journeys have taken him to every continent, except Antarctica. Alongside his passion for exploration, he indulges in various cultural activities, immersing himself in music and culinary delights from diverse corners of the world.

In addition to his appreciation for different cultures, Derrick has a profound interest in science fiction, particularly time travel, and non-fiction genres, especially technology and space travel. He also delves into subjects like Futurism and the profound influences artificial intelligence has on human civilization.